EDWARD SLEDGE

Ricardo's Collisions

ISBN: 978-0-57-893154-8

Advisor: Christina Sledge
Cover art by Hampton Lamoureux TS95 Studios

This book was professionally typeset on Reedsy.
Find out more at reedsy.com

Contents

THE DESIRE FAMILY SAGA: PART ONE

Edward L. Sledge Jr.
with Christina S. Sledge

Dedication & Playlist

Dedication

This book is dedicated to our daughters, family, friends, and all who support and purchase our books. To all the families, friends, and victims affected by drugs, especially by the crack era. To all the families, friends, and victims affected by domestic violence. To all the families, friends, and victims affected by gun violence.

To Antonio "Powerful" Madeam. Continue to rest in power, our brother.

Playlist

"Come & Talk to Me" by Jodeci
"I Wanna Sex You Up" by Color Me Bad
"All the Places (I Will Kiss You)" by Aaron Hall
"All Cried Out" by Lisa Lisa & The Cult Jam
"Secret Rendezvous" by Karyn White
"Saturday Love" by Alexander O'Neal and Sherrelle
"For the Love of Money/Living for the City" by Queen Latifah, Levert & Troop
"Never Keeping Secrets" by Babyface
"Goodbye Love" by Guy

"I Can Love You" by Mary J. Blige & Lil' Kim

"Set It Off" by Big Daddy Kane

"Shook Ones, Pt. II" by Mobb Deep

"Can I Live" by Jay-Z

"Just to Get a Rep" by Gangstarr

"Survival of the Fittest" by Mobb Deep

"Feenin'" by Jodeci

"Not Gon' Cry" by Mary J. Blige

"Ex-Factor" by Lauryn Hill

"Quiet Storm (feat. Lil' Kim)" by Mobb Deep & Lil' Kim

"Be Happy" by Mary J. Blige

"In the Air Tonight" by Phil Collins

I

Part One

Ricardo

BANG! Shot him in his chest, ripping through his heart. She stood there looking down at him and said, "Pierre Desire, I love you."

Character List

Ricardo: *Main character/narrator*
Pierre: *Ricardo's father*
Barbara: *Ricardo's girlfriend*
Tracy: *Ricardo's wife*

Chapter One

SLAM!

Oh shit! I can't believe this is happening to me. I remember my father once told me to watch out for the people who I love the most because those are the ones who will hurt me, and I think he was right. I am lying on this cold floor bleeding out. I can't seem to get up, and no one can hear me scream for help. Shit, I can barely talk, but I have to get up and grab the phone off the kitchen counter or else I'm going to die here. I have so much to live for and at the same time so much to be killed for. I should've stayed where I was at and never told anyone I was back in Brooklyn, but I had to. I have gained love and lost love, and I only blame myself. My only sins were being in love with two women and lying to both of them. Fuck it! I deserve to lie here and die.

I was born and spent most of my childhood in a wealthy suburb outside of Port-au-Prince, Haiti, where my father lived, but I spent my young preteen years in another wealthy suburb near Santo Domingo in the Dominican Republic where my mother was born and raised. When I was a child in Haiti, my father, who was the ministry of defense, had a lot of money. Most of the top government officials were wealthy, and that was because they were stealing from their citizens, even going as far as having criminals work for them and performing home invasions. They were dirty officials, and the citizens hated them. My father used to call the citizens who fought and rebelled against the government "horrible people." But in reality, my father and his government friends were the horrible people. I heard stories as a young boy of government officials' children as young as three years old being kidnapped and sometimes left on the streets dying as the horrible people cheered on. It was a scary time. We used to drive through the poor countryside. My father would stop the car, and while we would observe the poor, he would shake his head, put on a devilish smile, and call them peasants.

My father was a tall, thin, handsome, and charming man that women threw themselves at. Women from the rich to the poor loved him, and if any woman gave him the opportunity, he took it. He had a gift that attracted my mother, who was a beautiful woman. I was an only child, and I grew up watching love and how a marriage should be. They constantly could not stop touching each other even though she knew he slept with other women. Shit, I knew. Then one day jealousy entered our lives and stopped his heart. On one beautiful and sunny spring afternoon when I was eleven years old, my father and I got out of his car and walked into the grocery store. As soon as we walked out, one of the pregnant women whom he was having an affair with walked up to him.

BANG!

Shot him in his chest, ripping through his heart. She stood there looking down at him and said, "Pierre Desire, I love you."

While I stood there in shock and crying, she slightly turned to me, pointed her gun—

BANG!

She shot me in my right arm. As I yelled for help and started running—

CLICK! CLICK! CLICK!

"I will find you! And I will kill you!"

I ran through the streets bleeding until I collapsed. I started to bleed out and thought I was going to die. Just like I'm doing now. Somehow I woke up in the hospital in Santo Domingo, and my mother was standing by my side. After that incident, she refused to live in Haiti ever again. My mother and her family, full of strong and beautiful women, raised me. Although they were tough as nails, they didn't know how to teach me to become a man. Instead, they taught me how to love and praise women. The constant saying was, "Ricardo. Always remember. To capture a woman, you must first understand a woman." Soon an uprising started near the city we lived in, and we fled to the United States.

In the early 1980s, we moved to the upper east side of Manhattan. I couldn't speak a word of English, so I worked on that every day before I entered into high school. I heard stories of immigrants, especially Haitians, having a hard time in New York. They were treated like shit, being called racist names and getting beat up, but I never had to go through that. First of all, we lived on the upper east side; second, I went to an affluent private high school; and finally, I looked exactly like a young Pierre Desire. Guys wanted to hang out with me, and girls loved being around me; however, I stayed by myself, and I didn't date girls. The reason I stayed by myself was because my mother looked at any girl who wasn't Dominican and who didn't have wealth and power as a thief. The first time she suspected that I liked a girl, she sat me down and said, "Ricardo, dear. A woman who doesn't have wealth or an influential family is nothing but a thief. A thief for our family wealth, influence, and your future children. Those young girls and women are peasants and well below our standards."

However, because she didn't understand a man's point of view, she couldn't possibly explain to me what to do when a man actually falls in love. In high school, I was a six-foot-two, 160-pound, thin-looking boy, and I didn't like that. My father was thin, and I wanted to pull away from being like him. One day during my junior year, I saw some guys on the football team coming out of the weight room. They weren't the biggest guys I had ever seen, but they were doing something I really wanted to do. One football player who was in one of my classes said to me, "Hey, Ric. You're a good-looking dude. If you put on some weight and some muscle, you can be a beast."

That's just what I needed to hear, and I became excited.

"Really? How can I do that?"

"Man, I'm the captain of the football team. I can do whatever the fuck I want to. Listen, come to the weight room every day on your lunch break and at least two hours after school. By next year, you'll be a monster."

I did exactly what he told me to do every day until I graduated, and I bulked up. Girls came after me at full speed, and I rejected them because I knew my mother would not approve. I stayed a virgin until I went to college.

When I graduated, I was valedictorian, and I enrolled into Columbia University in Manhattan for law. I guess because of my experience with my father's murder, I wanted to understand the law and protect people. I was in my first class on the very first day and I saw the most beautiful woman I had ever seen. I sat directly behind her, and her perfume drove me nuts. She had to feel the breath from my nose on her neck, and I believed she enjoyed it. She was gorgeous and pure sexy, and that intimidated me. One day we were partners for a case study, and I just stared at her, and she caught me several times. There I was acting nervous and shy around her. In class, I daydreamed about her so much that I actually got a C in that class that semester. I followed her for a whole year before I ever said a word to her. Then one day she caught me staring at her and we locked eyes, so I had to walk to her and say something.

"I've been watching you for a year now."

"I know. I think it's cute."

"My name is Ricardo Desire, and you are going to be—"

"Your wife, and I'm thrilled about that."

I was trying to play it off even though I, too, was completely thrilled.

"What are you talking about? What makes you believe you're the one?"

She looked into my eyes with her beautiful brown eyes.

"Because we lust for each other. You're my Mr. Desire."

She smiled and at the same time was so serious, and it completely turned me on.

From that day, we became inseparable. For that whole year, we couldn't keep our hands and bodies off each other. Just making love in her dorm room while her roommate heard it and was turned on turned us on. We met every day in the same stall in the women's bathroom as she sneaked me in and I turned her around, placed my head under her skirt, and ripped her panties off, tasted her until we needed each other, then I picked her up, and after going up and down against the side of the wall, we exploded. We loved those moments. Then during our last semester of our senior year, we became pregnant, and we decided we weren't going to keep our baby. She was my first, and I learned so much about life being with her. She taught me how to expand my thinking of people, different cultures, and embrace New York City. We were so much in love, we held hands and loved being together. I found happiness, but I couldn't tell anyone about it, and she couldn't either. I felt we were placed dead smack between love and hate. We both grew up without fathers in our homes; therefore, we couldn't understand the love that a man feels for a woman and a woman understanding how a man totally in love feels. When we talked about the reasons behind our decision, it tore us apart. We still couldn't stop touching each other, but we had to discuss our next steps. A week later after making our decision, we were sitting on a park bench, and she looked at me.

"All right. The reason I chose not to have our baby is because I don't think we can manage a child right now before starting our careers. Tell me Ricardo. What is the reason behind your decision?"

I couldn't tell her the truth that my family was wealthy and that we could have a nanny take care of our child. That would have encouraged her to keep our baby. I kept her in the dark and never talked about my family, especially my mother. When we went places, we stayed near campus or far from my family. I never met any of her family members, and that was because she didn't think they would understand being in love while in college and making the same mistakes her sister did. And I surely couldn't tell her about how my mother felt about women. My mother would have embarrassed me and called the love of my life a greedy fucking peasant. Because no one in my life prepared me for this moment, I said the only thing I could think of. I moved my eyes from looking at her beautiful brown eyes, and I looked down at the floor.

"Because of the lives we live, I don't think we would have stayed together."

"You fucking bastard! You really don't see a future with me? And because of the lives we live? You know what, this isn't you talking. You don't have to say it. It's our families. I get it."

She stood up, bent over, placed her lips on my lips with a long kiss, and walked away. We officially broke up. I couldn't face seeing her again, so I let her go. We were pawns in a world of strong women who believed in love but didn't trust the world they fell victims to. We just had to move on, and within a week, I moved to Brooklyn. Instead of going into law, I applied to and became associate general counsel of a meat manufacturing company.

Being in that position was a great experience for me because I met so many new people and it took my mind off the woman I loved. After two weeks, the company hired a new assistant for my department, and there she was, a sexy tall White blonde whom I couldn't stop looking at. She stole my mind, and I felt an importance in my life again. After weeks of playing around and following her, I decided I needed to talk to her, so I walked up to her desk.

"Excuse me. I don't want to be rude, but you are one of the most beautiful women I have ever seen."

She looked up at me and smiled.

"For a fine man who could have any woman he wanted, you sure do a lot of stalking."

"Stalking?"

"I've been watching you watching me, and to be honest, every afternoon I daydream about you grabbing me by my arm, taking me into the storage closet, tearing my clothes off, and having your way with me. Anything you wanted to do, you did it."

"Wow. I thought about trying to have babies with you."

"Mr. Desire. I need you to place me on your bed and fuck me like you need me. I want my panties in your mouth when you are about to explode with my legs wrapped around your back."

I thought to myself, damn. I never had this told to me before, and when we got together that night, I had her wet red silk panties in my mouth as we were moaning. A few weeks later she became Mrs. Desire, and we desired each other all the time. We fucked at the job, on my desk, on the women's bathroom sink. Man, we put it on each other for years. But she was a jealous woman, and it got on my nerves. She once confronted me as soon as I arrived home.

"I know wherever you go, women want you, and I know you want them! Don't fuck them. Don't even talk to those bitches."

But I wasn't about that because I was always a one-woman man. I understood why she would think like that, shit, I looked exactly like Pierre, but I wasn't raised like that. I never told her I was not a player because Pierre was one and he was killed by a woman he had an affair with. I was faithful to my wife. We had a daughter, and three years later we had a son. I loved being the man Pierre wasn't until one company family picnic I saw a woman that I couldn't resist. She arrived with her husband, who was one of my employees, so I couldn't cross the line, but I wanted her and had to have her. We noticed each other from across the field, locking eyes, and we couldn't stop. I was a happily married man, and I wanted her badly. She was my first love, the one who left me at a park bench, and I still craved to see her face. I hated that she was married, especially to a loser like her husband. The sad part was I only could see her once a year at the picnic, but I thought about caressing and fucking her brains out all the time. I thought about her even while I was having sex with my wife. Yes, I thought about licking every place on that woman's body while I was making my wife orgasm. I think my wife knew I was thinking about another woman, but she never said anything. I followed my first love a lot. I followed her on her job, watched her arrive home, and I even studied her husband's work schedule and movements just to know things to say to throw his ass under the bus when I was ready to make my move. Ironically, I knew I wasn't that kind of guy, and I sure didn't want to be. I loved my wife, but lusting over my first love overwhelmed me. Both were my addictions and my temptations.

After a few times where I popped up at her job, we locked eyes and seduced each other for old times' sake, and that led to me missing work and giving excuses to my wife. Then it happened. One day we finished having sex, still naked, and she headed toward the bathroom. She went straight to look at herself in the hotel mirror, fixing her hair. Then I stood up and attacked her by holding her tight from behind and sticking everything I had inside her wet and warm goodness. She orgasmed, and I knew I captured her like she had captured me. Our lives changed. While lying down staring into her glossy eyes and my hand holding her hip toward me, I asked, "What's wrong?"

"Ricardo, I'm pregnant, and I'm keeping it."

"We are keeping it."

"We can't do this. I'm married and you're married."

I gave her a shocked look.

"How did you know that?"

"You beautiful man. I know about your wife. I talk to her every year at the picnics."

To keep her in my life, I lied.

"What people don't know is that we are getting divorced within a few months. Also, I'm applying for a position at work as a senior VP, and I will need to travel three days out of the week."

"Really? That's wonderful, but I still can't leave my husband."

"You don't have to, but I can't let you go."

She had a disappointed look on her face.

"He will know that I'm pregnant, and if it is a boy, we will have to name him after my husband."

"Anything to keep you in my life."

We slowly kissed and fucked again.

That night I told my wife that I was applying for the senior VP position, which meant I lied to both women, but to keep both women in my life, I had to. Of course, I had no intentions at all of leaving my wife. My wife was taking care of business at home, keeping me extremely satisfied. Damn. I remember a time in the middle of the day. She came into my office, closed the blinds, ripped open her dark blue blouse, losing her buttons everywhere, exposing her hard nipples barely sticking out over the top edge of her red satin bra, lifted up her skirt, pulled off her sexy purple lace panties, sat on my desk with her legs cocked up, placed her soft fingertips in my mouth, and softly said, "Kiss them first, then kiss these lips down here."

Once I did that, she climaxed, then after shaking, she turned over, and I thrust inside her wet lips, and she climaxed again on my shirt. The problem was neither of us had a change of clothes, so we had to wait in my office until four o'clock when we sneaked out. We kept each other empty.

Chapter Two

My wife lacked what my first love, Barbara, had. As a matter of fact, they both lacked what the other had. Barbara was educated and spoke proper, and I loved that. It was amazing, since we could talk for hours about the law. However, she lacked the emotion of loving a man who was in love with her. We both were having our cake and eating it too. Although she and her husband were having issues in their marriage, my job was to make sure to give her all the long, steamy sex she had to have.

My wife, Tracy, was excellent in the bedroom and anywhere else. She kept me empty, but what she lacked were two things. One was she lacked an education, but that wasn't her shortcoming I really complained about. The main one was having my mother hate her not only because she was a peasant, but my wife had a very raw vocabulary like three drunken sailors. She never backed down from my mother, calling her an old Hispanic piece of shit living in her great American country, and that didn't sit well with my mother or me. They didn't like each other when I first introduced them before we were married. My mother insisted that my wife didn't take our last name. To be spiteful to my mother, my wife made sure our kids took her maiden name. That burned my mother up. I was always in the middle of their arguments, and I hated that. We argued a lot about my mother and Tracy's foul mouth. The last time it happened I finally broke down.

"Why do you talk this way? As a gorgeous woman, it's not sexy to hear you talk like this."

"Well, motherfucker, stop being a polite, quiet, fucking mommy's boy, and stand up for me. Fucking punk! You are too big and too fucking sexy to not have a fucking spine."

Most importantly, the major problem was us not meeting each other before I met Barbara. As I said before, my sins were loving and lying to both women. One afternoon I was with Barbara in a hotel room, and she was distraught. She was so sexy being naked and eight months pregnant. While I was kissing and licking on her neck thinking about our next position, she said, "I have to tell you something."

"What is it, baby?"

"We have to stop this. I'm in love with you and my husband, and I can't take it anymore. I'm not leaving him, and you're not leaving Tracy."

"Then what's our next move? What are you thinking we should do?"

I definitely agreed that we both couldn't get divorced, and until I got serious and divorced my wife, I couldn't continue putting pressure on her.

"Look, Ric. You will always have the opportunity to see your son, but me and my husband need time to grow again as a couple. Yes, he is far from perfect, and there isn't any part of me that lusts for him, but he's still my husband. I owe him that much."

It was another hurtful moment in our relationship, but I understood. I just needed time to figure out how to stay in her life, and I knew it would be the new senior VP position to do it.

She turned around and looked at me.

"We have to stop this today." She stood her sexy pregnant ass up, walked across the room toward the couch, lifted up her right leg with her red high heel on the cushion, then turned her head around. "But first, come taste and get all this good loving!"

I couldn't resist. I walked up to her, roughly moved her hair to the side, kissed the back of her neck, thrusted my rock hardness up in her, and as soon as she gave the first moan, I bent her over, fucking her slowly as she was biting on the top of the couch pillow moaning and letting herself get to a place until her body stopped shaking and she became stiff and stuck, all the while staring back at me from the corner of her eyes. Man, just thinking about that moment, although I'm bleeding out dying, I am rock hard, damn!

Three years went by, and we never kept in touch. I was still thinking about her and my son, and all the while her husband was still one of my employees. My wife and I were still doing what we did, and yes, her vulgar vocabulary didn't change. It was a new era of drug addiction in the late eighties, and I wasn't letting it suck me in. A few of my employees and employees from other departments stopped coming to work, and I don't know exactly why, but it barely bothered me. I heard through the grapevine that my first love and her husband were breaking up. He stopped coming to work and barely went home to her, and that was my opening. I reached out to her and instantly became a super scumbag; I was turning into Pierre. I called her and told her that I started my new position, and she told me that not only did her husband leave her, as he became a drug addict, but that she had several relationships, and the latest one ended violently. We talked and agreed that I would be a great presence, being a kind, loving man for my son and his brother.

Because she lost her husband's income, she had to move, and man, she and her boys lived in a real shithole. She was a proud woman who never took a handout, and since I never informed her about my family's wealth, she would have questioned how I would have gotten the money to support her and the boys. I knocked on the door, and she opened it.

"Oh my gosh! You're finally here. Please come in and sit down. The boys are in school now, so make yourself comfortable. I'm going to change into something sexy."

She quickly ran into her bedroom. I stood there looking at her horrible apartment. As soon as I walked in, it smelled like a real shithole. I sat down on the couch, waiting for her to come out of the bedroom, and after two minutes, I put my hand in my pocket to check something in my wallet, and I felt the feeling of a creepy light breeze on my arm. I looked down, and there was an army of ants all over my left side. I jumped up, wiped them off, and when she came out, I was standing in the kitchen refusing to sit down again. She came out, grabbed my hands, placed them around her waist, walking backward toward the couch. I quickly picked her up, turned us around, and fucked her on the countertop. Later I told her I was buying her a new couch.

I stayed with them three days a week, and I stayed with my wife and family the other four days. I think my wife knew I really didn't have a new position. She hinted at the point that she knew I was lying to her. After we fucked in the shower, she dried off, then lay on the bed. I quickly had no choice but to kiss her lower lips, then turn her over and drive her crazy again.

When we finished, she turned around, placed her head on the pillow, kept her legs open, and looked at me.

"Ric. I know you really are not traveling all the time. But I understand the shit I put you through, and you're a mommy's boy. I put two and two together, and I know you stay at your mother's house for a few days. I get it and it's fine."

I thought that was perfect because she wouldn't call my mother's home and she wouldn't stop by there. Shit, my mother slammed the phone on her all the time. But just in case, I knew I would have to inform my mother and her servants that if my wife or kids called, tell them I was out. I nodded my head to my wife and I happily continued tasting her.

The boys never knew I had a son with Barbara; in fact, their mother and I agreed that no one would know. Therefore, when I did stay with them, they just knew I was their mother's new boyfriend. The oldest was twelve, and my son was nine, and they loved me, and I loved them. I treated them the same, and she loved that I did that. We went to sports games often, and I took them to museums. My goal was to make them feel comfortable around me. I enjoyed being with both women and both families, and I saw no possible way of me being caught between my two lives. A couple of times I thought I saw different men who were possibly former lovers of Barbara lurking around her building and even following us, so I always stayed aware, but nothing ever came about it. Until...

SLAM!

"You still alive, Ric? Huh?"

I'm trying to ask this person for help, but I lost my voice. I turn my head to the left while choking on my own blood.

"Oh shit! Why are you doing this?"

BANG!

II

Part Two

James

POW! She slapped me. "Boy. Don't you ever talk to me like that ever in your life again. You're my child, I'm not yours. I love that man..."

<u>Character List</u>

James: Main character/narrator
Barbara: James's mother
Greg Sr.: James's father
Michael, **Daniel** & **Diane**: James's friends
Greg Jr.: James's brother
Ricardo: Barbara's boyfriend
Percy: James's friend
Carol: James's aunt
Olena & **Tiffany**: James's cousins
Kenya: James's girlfriend

Chapter Three

I have been in this supermarket for fifteen minutes trying to comprehend what is about to happen when I walk out the door. Ten minutes ago, this guy I knew came in and "accidentally" saw me, we exchanged greetings, we shook hands, and then we hugged each other. After small talk, I told him I would come across the street when I was finished shopping. I knew him and his friends for a few years, but they were never my friends. We ran the streets together doing small crimes, but now he's setting me up. But I don't know why.

As soon as he left, I felt a strong, eerie feeling, the one a person gets when they know it's about to go down. It's the "This is the beginning of my final days on earth" kind of feeling. I felt this way before when I was arrested and walked into a jail cell of nobodies.

After he left, I called one of my friends, and he didn't answer. Then I called another friend, and he said he would take at least an hour and a half to reach me because he was at work. The one friend I can call and definitely can depend on turned his life around years ago, and I can't let him help me because it will destroy his family if he gets hurt.

My heart is racing, thoughts going fast, survival rate is low, and I'm running out of options. If I go out the back door, someone might be waiting, but I can't stay in this store forever. I don't have any help or any protection on me, and if this is the end, the guy who shook my hand either knew I didn't have protection or thought I was going out in a blaze. I did so many crazy things in my twenty-seven years that I knew this day would come. I'm not leaving until my friends call or texts me back. Damn! How did this happen?

I had a happy and stable childhood. I was born in Brooklyn, New York, to a young Black couple who was just a few months into their marriage. My mother, Barbara, was a beautiful Black woman who attracted men. She had a Coke bottle body, and she was extremely smart. She went to college in New York at Columbia University and became an adjunct law professor. My father's name is Greg, and he was a good-looking, tall, and muscular man who favored George Foreman in his prime, and he was a ladies' man. Everyone in the neighborhood knew him, since he didn't take any shit and he punched out a few guys. He was not educated, but he wasn't a dumb man either. They met one day while waiting for the A-train in the Crown Heights section in Brooklyn as he approached her. Although he was a ladies' man, he never cheated on my mother.

He worked at a meat-packing company. Every year the company had its annual picnic, and when we went, I hung out with Michael and Daniel, who were boys my age and who happened to live on my block. Michael was a rough, edgy boy who just couldn't sit still, and Daniel was quiet and kind of shy. Our parents hung out all the time and were really tight. But at the end of every picnic, my father would always end up arguing with some coworkers and once with a manager who was looking at my mother. My parents loved each other so much, and on my third birthday, I was told they were having another baby, my little brother, Greg.

We lived in a rented brownstone in Brooklyn, and every Saturday night their friends came over and partied using cocaine. However, the company started laying off many employees, and even though my father wasn't one of them, my family was impacted. Several of my parents' friends were laid off, and several nights they came over to eat with us, and my parents sometimes gave them money to get by, causing financial strains and heated arguments between my parents. One night their argument got so heated that they threw plates with food at each other, smashing the walls. However, they also loved hard, and hearing those times made me feel happy because I knew they would stay together. And then crack infested our neighborhood and life changed.

I was eight years old when I first experienced the negative impact crack had on my environment. My mother never smoked crack; however, it hit my father and his friends big-time. It hit Michael's and Daniel's fathers first, probably because they didn't have jobs, being part of the group laid off. Daniel's pops started selling crack and started making big-time money, even selling to Michael's parents. He started selling because he needed to make some money for his family of four. Michael's father smoked crack and never looked back. He was quickly hooked and looked bad all the time. His family depended on him for everything. Rumor has it that he started smoking crack after he was smoking weed that was laced with crack with a friend and Michael's pops didn't know it. He then did the same thing to his wife so they could share something together. She was completely hooked. He had her selling her body to friends, neighbors, and drug dealers. It was horrible, and Michael and his younger sister moved into their grandmother's house a block away from where they lived.

I started witnessing my father coming home later than usual, and he soon missed work a lot, and they fired him for not showing up. Many times my mother was yelling at him because money was missing from her purse and even from the joint bank account. His stealing was so bad that one day he broke down their bedroom door because she put a lock on it to keep him out while she was at work. I began missing toys because he stole and sold them. And at a few Christmases, the toys I had gotten from my mother were taken by him, especially a Louisville Slugger baseball bat I begged my mother for.

He was still a big and scary man, so he used his strength and robbed people, either grabbing their gold chains and running or punching them out. He started hanging with Michael's parents and a skinny White woman who was also a crack addict. Michael, Daniel, and I used to see all four of them begging for money, breaking into cars, and selling stolen things. We would quickly take the back streets through the alleys to avoid them walking home from school.

Those few years stressed my mother out to the point where she had to take weeks off at a time for health reasons. My mother was losing her hair at the same time my father was losing his teeth. When people talked about the crack era, I never saw cameras focusing on what happens to the families. Our families broke down and never recovered. We loved my father through all the pain, the middle-of-the-night sleeping on the hard, stinking wooden benches in different parks around Brooklyn, and the loss of stolen rent money. My mother was a strong and proud woman who would tighten her belt before she asked for any help. My grandmother wanted to pay the rent and take care of me and my brother. She begged my mother to get a divorce, but my mother didn't hit rock bottom as of yet. My mother loved her family but loved my father even more, hoping to help him turn around.

By ten years old, I started liking girls, and there was this one very pretty girl in my class who lived on my block named Diane who I knew liked me. I would be in class and just daydream about her. She was special. We talked just like a brother-sister relationship, but there were many times I saw her looking at me. Diane started walking home with me, Michael, and Daniel because she knew all of us. She, too, was traumatically impacted by the crack epidemic, since her mother became a crack addict and was out there being chased by police, and by her father struggling to save his wife's life.

One day we all walked home from school and took the same alleys we normally did. We saw Daniel's pops standing up with his head leaning back against the wall behind a dumpster. Another person was there on their knees hiding behind the dumpster; we could see the soles of their black sneakers on their feet sticking out from the other side behind the dumpster. We all stopped, as Daniel was extremely embarrassed, and Diane started crying because she remembered hearing her father talk about her mother getting caught by him several times performing sexual acts. Diane wanted to turn back, but I didn't want to run into my father and his friends. So as soon as we were about to turn around, the person on the ground got up, at the same time wiped their lips, turned, and looked at us, and it was my father, Greg.

Chapter Four

As I stood there in that supermarket thinking about that moment, a cold and firm hand landed on my right shoulder.

"Sir. Sir! Do you need some help finding something?"

It was a supermarket employee.

"No. I'm sorry. I'm just waiting for my wife to text me the type of corn she wants. I can't go home with the wrong kind. All hell would break loose."

He looked at me with an understanding husband's look.

"I definitely understand, sir. Just find me if you need help."

As he walked away, I realized both of my friends haven't called or texted me back yet. I can't keep walking around this store for too much longer.

After that moment in the alley, I felt so ashamed that I couldn't tell my mother; however, Diane told her father, and he informed my mother, and that was her rock bottom. I never blamed Diane for that, but we never looked at each other the same. I stopped daydreaming about her, and I really pulled away from talking to her because I never knew if I could trust her with any of my secrets. My mother threw my father out of the house for good, and she had to recover fast, but it wasn't that easy. She was still a woman fighting what life was throwing at her, including the mental and financial obstacles in a cold, new world. She cried a lot but never in front of us. We didn't see our father in the next two years, and the last time we did, he was hiding in our lobby wearing a dirty, torn white T-shirt with dirty cut-off jean shorts. He didn't even say hello as he ran right past us, taking the door off the hinges and leaving his burned chicken bone he used to smoke crack with on the ground.

During those years I started to become independent and helping out around the house, especially since my mother didn't come home until around six o'clock. I cooked for me and Greg, and our favorite dish was mac and cheese because boiling water was easy. During that time, I saw my mother date four men. The first guy was an older man she worked with at Columbia named Louis Franks. He was a good guy, kind of overweight, had an education, but he tried too hard trying to play daddy to us. After three weeks, he came to our apartment, slammed the door, and yelled, "James. Greg. Daddy's home!"

My mother looked at him and shook her head.

"Don't do that, Lou."

"Look! I need to be a father to our sons. They need a strong male in their lives."

"Lou! These are not your sons. We're not getting married! You need to rethink what's going on here."

After weeks of Greg and I giving him the cold shoulder, he got the hint and moved on without saying goodbye. The second idiot's name was Kevin Boothman, and he had no chance with us. He lived with us for two weeks, but he was scared. He always was looking around in the street hoping my father wouldn't come up and beat his ass. We heard him talking to my mother one late night. She was trying to convince him that everything was safe and that he shouldn't worry about my father. Kevin didn't want to be seen in public with her because he thought my father would beat him up.

"Kevin. I really like you, but my husband is not coming to get you."

"Are you sure? He's a big man."

Yep, scared-ass Kevin didn't last long. He was even bigger and taller than my father. Those two came and they went, but the third one, Mark Walkens, really made his mark on our family.

Mark was a dark-skinned man from the neighborhood who was tall and muscular and was one of the many men waiting for my parents' marriage to break up. He was an older street dude who used to run the streets with a lot of dangerous criminals. Mark used to beat my mother at least once every two weeks like clockwork. He used to beat her so badly, but she never reported it or went to the hospital for her injuries. She wore a lot of makeup, but everyone knew what was happening to her, and nobody spoke up, until one night I found the courage to get involved. That night I was standing at the stove getting ready to make mac and cheese, and she came home from work around six o'clock. Mark was already at our place because he "lost" his job as soon as he met my mother. It was a cold and rainy night when she came in. She was already mad because the lazy bastard took and hid her umbrella to mess with her that morning. She was soaking wet, and as she was taking off her coat, she looked over at him.

"Are you going to take my coat and hang it up?"

I knew right there he was going to snap her neck. My mother never talked to him like that. My mother was a strong woman, but she didn't have the courage to have him locked up. He got his lazy ass off her couch, walked toward her, and back smacked her so hard that she went backward and fell into the refrigerator door.

"Bitch! Don't you ever talk to me like that again ever in your life. You got some fucking nerve."

As he was walking toward her, I grabbed the butcher knife and ran toward him. He moved out of the way, and I missed him, and when I quickly turned around, he punched me dead on my nose, breaking it. While his back was turned, my mother and Greg jumped on him, and I took the huge pot of boiling water and threw it on him. He started yelling and screaming,

"MOTHERFUCKER! MOTHERFUCKER!"

He was running around, bumping into the walls, knocking down the television and stereo, then my mother hit him in the head two times with the heavy weight bar I used for working out, and Mark collapsed and passed out. We called the cops, and they came and arrested him. My mother and Greg also were hit with the hot water, my mother on her wrist and Greg on the back of his leg near his foot. The cops took us to the hospital to address their injuries. That moment made me realize I crossed the line into a new world of violence. And if I needed to, I could do it again. Unfortunately, Mark only served that night in jail and was probably waiting to get revenge on us or any of her future boyfriends.

"Sir? Do you need some help? You look kind of dazed."

I looked up, and I saw an employee who was a young White man who probably stocked the shelves.

"No. I'm fine. I'm just sitting here waiting for a call. Taking a break from walking."

Come to think about it, why haven't I received a call yet? Shit! I can't get a signal in this section of this sorry-ass supermarket that is ironically keeping me alive for now. I have to get back on my feet and keep moving around until I get a signal.

Ricardo was the best boyfriend she ever had. We all loved him, especially Greg. We really wanted them to get married so he could be a stepfather to us. He and my mother had a strong chemistry. It was sort of like watching our parents when we were younger, before my father fell victim to the crack epidemic. My mother and Ricardo complemented each other. Greg and I sat around them as they talked about the thing they loved more than themselves being a couple, and that was the law. My mother, who was an adjunct law professor, taught criminal justice, and her stories fascinated Ricardo and us. They gave each other feedback on basically how to get away with any crime, especially murder. It was like they were in sync with the minds of serial killers and the cold cases that were never solved. I was intrigued. They laughed with each other, they never argued, and man, they definitely weren't shy about how happy couples have fun in the bedroom.

At first it sucked hearing their lovemaking because we didn't know if Ricardo was going to be another two-to-three-week romance, but with him, we were glad he made her happy, which made us happy. Also, it made me feel that was the way to love a woman. Unfortunately, my father never had the chance to explain the birds and the bees to me, and my mother didn't have the opportunity because she was working and dealing with life herself. Luckily, I wasn't out in the world like that. I was a virgin and was afraid of getting a girl pregnant or repeating the events I witnessed in my parents' relationship. I didn't understand adult shit, the complex lives people have behind their smiles and frowns. I didn't want to experience chasing my wife down in the streets hoping she would stop selling herself for a drug that was so addictive that it caused actions that ordinary people would have been embarrassed of but a crack addict didn't even think twice about. The stories Diane, Michael, and Daniel told were more horrible than mine, but they said they never wanted to be in my shoes. So, without him giving me the birds-and-bees talk, which I knew he would do one day, Ricardo's actions made me want to become a man. Therefore, we accepted him in our lives. We called him dad, and that definitely closed the door on our father's chapter in our lives. Even our friends embraced Ricardo.

He was educated, and he changed our lives forever. He worked at the same company my father did, but Ricardo traveled two to three days per week. Ironically, I think he was one of the workers my father used to argue with because he was watching my mother at those phony-ass company picnics. He was another of those guys who was waiting for my parents' marriage to end. But he was totally different from the others, especially when we got to know him. Ricardo came into our lives when I was twelve years old. He was Dominican, and he made a lot of money. He had one of the latest BMWs, so we always drove to places. He took us to baseball games. We sat in either the expensive first-row seats behind the dugout or behind home plate, and after every game, we met the players. He educated us about life and different cultures and took us to different museums and even amusement parks. Everywhere we went, he was well respected and embraced by people who knew him. He treated my mother with love and respect, and we all felt protected around him. He was a breath of fresh air to us every day, even when we didn't go out to a game or out to eat; the moments we spent with him felt exciting and were just what my mother needed. Because he mostly was on the road for work, the times he was home, it was all about us, nothing work related ever came up. It was two fantastic years he was in our lives when disappointment arrived, as what goes up has to sometimes fall down. Like every man that came before him, he also disappointed us.

One Sunday late afternoon after a Mets game, we were driving home, and Greg asked if we could stop to get something to drink because he was very thirsty. Ricardo was scheduled to leave for the road that night, and he wanted to spend more time with us, so we stopped. There weren't any close parking spots, so we had to park two blocks away. We got something for Greg to drink, grabbed three ice cream cones, and started walking back to the car. It was a beautiful sunny day for the perfect storm that was about to hit us. While we were walking to the car, Greg looked at Ricardo.

"We know you and our mother love each other. Are you going to ask her to marry you?"

I knew that couldn't happen because my mother was still married, and I believed Ricardo knew it too. He looked at Greg.

"I wouldn't wish for anything more in the world than to marry your mother."

Then we heard a woman's voice.

"Hey, Ric. What are you doing down here?"

We looked, and there was a very beautiful White woman standing in front of him. He said hello to her and quickly looked at us.

"And who are these good-looking boys?"

He looked at her and cracked a smile.

"This is James and his younger brother, Greg."

"Wow. Hi there. These are some handsome nephews you have here. My name is Renee."

I thought Ricardo was going to correct her about us being his nephews, but in reality, he wasn't our father, and although he treated us like his own, he wasn't technically our stepfather.

And with men coming in and out of our lives, I didn't feel bad that he didn't claim us.

"Well, Ric. Let me go now. I'll tell Tracy that I ran into you and your handsome nephews. I'll see you tomorrow night."

She kissed him on the cheek and walked away. He stayed quiet the whole way home. Why and how would he see her tomorrow when he was scheduled to leave town for work that night? Also, who was Tracy? We knew that Ricardo was an only child, so we couldn't be his nephews. We arrived home and told our mother about the game.

"We met Renee today. And for some reason she said that Ricardo was going to see her and Tracy tomorrow night," Greg said.

"What the hell are you talking about, Greg?"

"I guess before he leaves for work."

My mother was livid as she looked at us.

"RICARDO! RICARDO! I know them. They are sisters who worked with your father and Ricardo at the meat company. I used to talk to them at the annual company picnics."

Ricardo came out of the room with the suitcases he traveled with for work. He stopped in front of my mother, who was standing at the front door with us behind him. If any bullshit was going down, we were tearing him up. No longer was any man hitting our mother.

"Ric. I love you to death, and if I could, I would get a divorce in a heartbeat and marry you. Tell me what Tracy has over me. I can't lose you, and you know you're the best man I ever had. You told me that you and Tracy separated, and you have been trying to have her sign the divorce papers! You were lying to me all this fucking time? For two years, Ric? Do you even have a traveling position at work?"

My mother became overwhelmed with shock and a surprised look like she solved a mystery. She placed her hands over her wide-open mouth.

"Oh shit! Of course, you don't. You've been fucking and staying with me and Tracy! For two years, Ric? I can't believe this shit."

Ricardo stared at her and said in a low, strong voice,

"I love you. I have loved you since I first saw you. We have history together. Time went by, and I fell in love with Tracy, and we got married and had two kids. I'm so sorry, but I couldn't fully leave my family. I'm so much in love with both of you."

"You motherfucker! Get all your shit and get the fuck out!"

Ricardo had no words for her. My mother ran past us and into her bedroom. She was crying and throwing things. He turned, looked at me and Greg, and said to us as he quietly cried, "Boys. I'm deeply sorry. I had no intentions of hurting both of you and definitely not your mother. Please don't carry any hate in your hearts for me. As you can see, we adults still can't get it together. Try to be your own man. When both of you come into your own, try to make the right decisions. It will be hard because life throws you curveballs, and at those moments, you probably will not know what to do. Hopefully we'll see each other again. I don't know if I can fix this, but I love you both and your mother."

"Can we call you? Visit you?" Greg asked Ricardo.

"I'm sorry, Greg. I wish I could, but your mother probably wouldn't want that, and my wife definitely wouldn't want that."

Then Ricardo turned and looked at me.

"James. I couldn't get you ready for the real world, especially with girls, and that's my fault. I thought I would have more time with you and Greg. But whatever you do, get your education, go to college, and lead the way for Greg. He is very smart and young. I'm depending on you to take care of my little man."

I thought to myself, how the hell am I going to do that? I still need assistance. Then Ricardo hugged us and kissed us on the top of our heads. He turned around, walked toward the door, opened it, and walked out of our lives. Reality set in when the door that took so long to close finally did. We loved that man. When he left, we all were stunned. My mother ran out her room and open the apartment door,

"Ricardo! Ricardo! Come back, Ricardo, please!"

She yelled his name as if she couldn't live without him. At that moment, I was confused, but now I fully understand. Soon she had a major breakdown. Because she felt so horrible about being lied to and losing her beloved Ricardo, she quit her job and started abusing pain medication. I stopped living with her because I couldn't take her just zoned out. I would be talking to her and looking right in her face, and she wouldn't respond. When I looked into her eyes, she was gone. I was tired of being alone around her, neglected, and watching her tap out on life. The moment that I realized I had to go came the night I came home and I saved her from overdosing. I called 911, and the paramedics came, saved her, and took her to the hospital.

Chapter Five

A few days after the incident at my house, Daniel told me he heard from his mother, who was still close to people working at Ricardo's job, that Tracy confronted Ricardo, kicked him out, and was filing for divorce. His double life took a huge toll on his family and my family. My mother stopped being the lively person she was and just worked and barely cooked or ate during the weeks after the breakup. One time I walked into her room and sat next to her on the edge of her bed while she was silently crying.

"Ma. What's wrong? Do you need me to find Ricardo? Tell him to call you? Bring him back to you? Beat the shit out of him?"

POW!

She slapped me. "Boy. Don't you ever talk to me like that ever in your life again. You're my child, I'm not yours. I love that man, and until you've been in love, you wouldn't know what the hell I'm going through."

"But, Ma. He cheated on you and lied. I don't have to be in love to understand that he's wrong."

"Boy. You really don't know shit. That man was stuck trying to choose between two beautiful women. I'm a grown-ass woman. I always knew the rules. I don't fault him because I knew better, but we love each other."

"Love, Ma?"

She looked at me with anger just because I asked that question.

"Yes, James! I still and always will love Ricardo. He is the greatest man I ever loved. Now, please leave my room."

From that conversation, Greg and I really had to raise ourselves. I couldn't blame her because she had been through a lot, especially since love and happiness always found a way to leave her. After the men I saw her with, I knew I wasn't ever doing drugs, hitting women, or never working a nine to five job because trouble and drama come from those environments. As the summer ended that year, Michael, Daniel, Diane, and I all were entering our first year of high school, and we met a junior who influenced our lives, and his name was Percy.

Percy was the man. He was two years older than us. I first saw him at my grandmother's surprise birthday party two years earlier when he was dating my older cousin Katrina. They were madly in love with each other. Throughout high school, they were off and on and secretly seeing each other, but they were true soul mates. Everyone in high school knew and embraced Percy. He knew and got along with almost everyone because he was approachable. He hung out with thugs. I mean guys that injured and murdered other dudes either with guns or knives. Guys he would call and would rain down firepower in a heartbeat. Percy was fearless, and if he was scared, you wouldn't ever know it. I took to him like a magnet. He wasn't a father figure but a mentor for me in the streets. He also experienced pain and suffering at an early age. He had his own place at fourteen years old. Michael and Daniel also took to Percy, but not like I did. He was too rough for them. Percy was hanging with people Daniel's pops were side partners with.

Daniel's pops said to us, "I heard y'all are hanging with that Percy dude. He is bad news. That dude is too much violence and drama for y'all. He is a real dude. A survivalist. He went through shit y'all young men couldn't even imagine. And he's only sixteen years old. Don't fuck with him. Say your hellos and goodbyes, smile, and keep it moving. No small talk and hope you stay on his good side. James, you should be good because he's in love with Katrina. But I can't stress it enough, stay away from him. If not, you're looking at prison or death."

I listened to Daniel's pops, but come on. Now he cares so much about us? He's probably still selling crack to my father and Michael's parents. I took well to Percy, especially since we didn't have any older men to teach us differently. He gave us courage to talk to girls and, most importantly, understanding the streets and surviving. He was always playing chess in his head, like he knew how and when to move at the right time. When anybody needed him, he dropped everything and went to them. Percy was becoming a street legend hanging with other street legends like T-Black, LB, Big-Face Horse, Pan-Head Ed, and Black Pu. He also hung around the intelligent minds such as Divine, Tumu, and the Powerful One.

RING! RING! RING!

Oh shit! Oh shit! My phone's ringing. Where's my phone?

"What's up, man? I've been trying to call you. I need your help now!"

"Man. I can't make it now. The guy who would have replaced me called out sick today."

"What do you mean you can't make it? I don't give a damn about your replacement. Every time you needed me, I was there. Now I need you and you can't come?"

CLICK!

Percy always said dudes might say they got you, but ninety-nine percent of them really don't. Damn, my other man just texted me that he's coming from New Jersey and is stuck in traffic on I-95. But I know that's bullshit. He has never been on a rescue mission before, which looks like it may turn into a shoot-out. He isn't coming, but I'll keep giving him the benefit of the doubt. Shit, I really don't have a choice.

The third week of school I finally met Percy. Michael, Daniel, and I were walking to school one morning, and Katrina was standing outside on the corner talking to her friends and waiting for Percy to show up. He barely went to school; however, he did so just to meet up with Katrina.

She saw us. "Hey, James, Michael, and Daniel. Stay here with me for a minute, I want to introduce y'all to Percy."

That was a dope moment for me. Meeting Percy was a highlight for us, so we waited. Katrina was always my favorite cousin. She was one of the few whom I could ever count on for advice with school, advice with how to plan to go to college, and being goal oriented. We all knew she was going to make something of herself one day. We wouldn't be shocked to say yep, we knew it would be her. Family and friends questioned why she was with Percy, but love is love, and the heart wants what it wants. I wasn't questioning that shit.

Katrina turned to us. "How's school going for all of you? I know freshman year can be demanding and at the same time exciting."

"So far it's good," said Michael, who always had a crush on her.

"Going to all your classes, correct?" Katrina asked.

We all said, "Yeah," at the same time, and then she said,

"Here comes the love of my life."

We turned around, and Percy was stopping and talking with everyone who knew him, and they embraced him—I mean from the nerds to the thugs—and he was walking toward us. He stopped at Katrina.

"Percy. This is my little cousin and his friends. They all are freshmen."

Percy shook our hands. "What's good people?"

He kissed Katrina. "Come on, Kat. Let me walk you to class."

I looked at Michael and Daniel, and I knew they didn't trust him.

Weeks later he and Katrina broke up. At that time, Percy and I started hanging together more and more. That meant I was in class less and less. He introduced me to his friends and to girls, and I introduced him to Diane one day. She was an honor student, a big-time nerd. She knew about Percy, and when they met, she was in awe. Michael, Daniel, and I started cutting classes, smoking, and going to parties in the middle of the school day. Many times I was scared and at the same time in survival mode. Michael, Daniel, and I didn't graduate, and I couldn't blame anyone but myself because I knew better.

Percy left and joined the air force. Really? He knew he was looking at prison or being killed in these streets. He knew his odds were turning low for survival. He used to always say that people who run toward a goal are usually running away from something. I never knew what he was running from.

Years went by, and the next thing I knew I turned twenty-one years old. Greg never tried following me around—he was always the smartest one and never followed in my footsteps. He wanted a better life for himself, and so he applied to colleges, and he got in one out of state, leaving me and my mother. I wasn't mad at him because I knew I couldn't offer him a better life. Even though he never showed it, he never accepted the way our mother couldn't get over her depression.

More years went by, and the next thing I knew, I turned twenty-seven years old, still living with my mother. I knew she needed help, someone to stay with her, and I really couldn't leave her, but I had to live my own life. Then one day she was in the kitchen sitting at the table, and I walked in from my room and sat next to her.

"Ma. I love you, but I am moving out."

She looked at me with a stone-cold stare and with a low, calm voice said,

"Then get the fuck out."

I got up, packed my things, and I knew right there that Ricardo leaving had taken more than my mother's body, mind, and soul—it had taken her life. I recognized she wanted to leave everything behind, even her sons, to be with Ricardo, and she was going to end her life very soon but in a slow way. She was lost and neglectful. My grandmother couldn't take my mother's suicide attempts anymore, and so she admitted her into a psychiatric ward with only her, my aunt Carol who was handling my mother's finances, Greg, and I allowed to visit her.

The family members on my mother's side were mostly women. They tried to teach and encourage me about working, finding a career, and discovering happiness. Sadly, I never listened. I vividly remember one time at my grandmother's home when I was twenty-one years old. My aunt Carol was there, and so were her two nineteen-year-old identical twin daughters, Olena and Tiffany. They went to colleges in the same state, and they were doing great in school. They were supersmart and beautiful girls. They were discussing Tiffany's and Olena's career paths of Tiffany not staying with her goal of becoming a surgeon. She wanted to be an EMS paramedic, and Olena also wanted to change her major from medicine to something else. My aunt Carol didn't like their reasoning for their change of mind. I rudely jumped into their conversation, and as one can imagine, she definitely didn't like it. As she was talking to them, I walked into the living room and interrupted.

"I think it's great that you want to be a paramedic. They save lives, especially before they get to the hospital. Don't become a surgeon, and you, Olena, you have to be a crime fighter. The world needs more of those."

My aunt Carol turned around and looked at me.

"And who the fuck are you? Why are you in our business? You don't have a pot to piss in or a window to throw it out of. You can't contribute anything to this conversation or even this world. Mind your own business, and focus on your own mother."

"Aunt Carol, I apologize. And I will focus on my mother's mental illness, who by the way is your sister."

My life was out of whack, and I didn't know how to fix it. I didn't even know how the bills were being paid. And then one evening in July while at my grandmother's house, I received a devastating call from Daniel. I picked up the phone.

"What's up, Daniel?"

"James! Ricardo was found dead this afternoon in his home."

"Ricardo was found dead today. What the hell are you talking about?"

"For real. The cops questioned Michael about it."

I was shocked. I couldn't imagine anyone other than my mother or his wife killing him.

"James. He committed suicide. Gun in hand. I can't believe

he would do that shit. I have to go. I'll call you back later."

"Let me know the details when you can. Damn."

As soon as we hung up, I received another call from Michael.

"Did Daniel tell you the news?"

"Yeah. Any more details?"

"Yep. Ricardo was found in his Brooklyn brownstone on the kitchen floor with a gunshot to his head and the gun in his hand as a suicide. That's all I know for now. I'm sorry, man. We loved him as much as you did."

"Thanks."

"I will call you once I find out more."

We hung up, and my world suddenly went into a different place. I didn't even know where he lived. I didn't know specifically what he was going through after I last saw him, but I heard he went missing off the face of the earth, and I couldn't see him committing suicide. However, later the word was that the crime scene looked like a set up. The detectives called the time of death around ten o'clock, and no arrest was made. I couldn't tell my mother, but my aunt Carol did, and at first, my mother took it as calmly as a person already in a depressed state would. Then she flipped out, and the staff had to sedate her. I informed Greg, who was already in Brooklyn for his college summer break, and we cried and cried. He took it hard.

A few days later my mother calmed down, and my aunt Carol talked the staff into letting my mother leave the hospital for a few hours under the promise she would return her back to the hospital so she could attend Ricardo's funeral. My aunt Carol, my mother, Greg, and I went to the funeral together, but aunt Carol stayed in the car parked two blocks away. The funeral home was packed, and we knew we were probably going to be looked at as the ones who destroyed their family and friendships with their beloved Ricardo. As soon as we walked in, Greg started crying, and he went into the bathroom, and my mother and I continued walking into the viewing room. We walked up to the casket. While we stood there, people were whispering, and we heard, "There's that money-hungry homewrecker bitch!"

My mother turned around and yelled over the low-playing organ music and other conversations, "I LOVED THIS MAN TOO. WE LOVED RICARDO. ALL OF Y'ALL JUST GO TO HELL!"

It was the first time I saw Ricardo's daughter and his son; however, I don't believe my mother saw Tracy there. My mother and I turned and left the room, and we ran into Greg standing outside the funeral home.

"I'm sorry, Ma. I just couldn't go in there and see him like that."

My mother hugged both of us. "I understand, but I had to see him. With our history, I definitely couldn't picture him lying in a casket."

We all started walking to aunt Carol's car and returned my mother to the hospital. I stayed with Daniel, and although he was one of my best friends, seeing his pops once in a while really made me angry, so then I moved in with my grandmother. After living with the women in my family, I started living with women I was dating. I met a woman named Kenya who was twenty-one. She worked as an assistant manager at a high-end clothing store in midtown Manhattan and already had an apartment and a young daughter around three years old. We met while waiting for the A-train, and when I saw her, I knew she was mine. I got a job as a janitor, and we did the living-together thing.

Kenya's daughter's father was a tough dude, but I wasn't a joke either, and I wasn't going to let him clown me to show her what she was missing. The first time I met him, he was trying to set the rules of engagement with me. Talking about I better not do this or do that. I pulled out my gun, cocked it back, and told him that I would put two hot ones in him. The next day he called the cops on me, and I was placed in Central Bookings for the weekend. That was the first time I was locked up, and I was scared but didn't show it. I walked in the huge, cold cell with maybe twenty dudes who had their own small groups. I quickly remembered what Percy told me. The streets are like jail. Your survival depends on your movements and who you know. I looked around and saw a crazy dude who once ran with Percy, and I survived. I came out, and days later I lost my job because I didn't show up, but I couldn't tell them why. My life was in shambles, and then I messed up and smacked Kenya while we were arguing over her daughter's punk-ass father. We had a lot of physical arguments, but for some sick reason, we stayed together like Mark and Barbara. I started not caring about the man looking back at me in the bathroom mirror.

Chapter Six

I hadn't seen my mother since the funeral, and Kenya and I were not happy. I didn't love her. Diane was the only girl I ever loved. I continued following in the footsteps of the males in my life, and I treated Kenya wrong by having affairs. I got a job as an apartment building assistant manager for a few buildings in Brooklyn. I met both single and married women, had sex with them, came home, and took a shower before Kenya came home. I got a woman pregnant, and I stole the rent money of another, blaming it on her teenage son. Then Kenya got pregnant, and I tried to change, but I couldn't. During what should have been a time of togetherness and embracing the moment, my jealousy and insecurity kicked in.

I was coming home one afternoon, and she and her daughter's father were outside talking. I understood they had to talk, but they looked too relaxed. Maybe it was because they decided to make peace and move on with their lives because getting back together wasn't an option. Maybe it was because I felt they shouldn't like each other but not enough to have war, or maybe because I was doing dirt and I didn't trust any man. Whatever the case, the animal side of me didn't like them talking to each other.

"Kenya. What was that about? What was going on?"

"Don't worry about it."

"Excuse me? Please tell me this is not his baby you're carrying?"

"What? You need to get your stuff out of my apartment now and leave."

I should have taken a breath and apologized, but in front of a crowd of people—

SLAP!

I smacked the living crap out of her. I looked at her, shook my head, and ran because with that smack, I was way beyond saying sorry. I had the possibility of being locked up again, which wasn't going to work for me, or have her brothers come for me, and I didn't have the bullets or the manpower to help me. I went to my grandmother's home and stayed there for three days. While I was there, I was talking to my grandmother, and she said someone that was not on the list tried to visit my mother. To my knowledge, no one knew where she was. Also, who and why did someone want to visit her? They had to know she was in there because of a mental breakdown, and she was probably drugged so much that she probably wouldn't recognize them. Maybe it was my father or Mark? Maybe to apologize for their sins? Repentance? I walked to my aunt Carol, and I was about to ask her, then my phone rang.

"Who is this?"

"My man. Come see me! I'm back in Brooklyn for a week."

I knew that voice.

"Oh shit! Percy, my brother. I would love to see you. I'll be at your pops' house ASAP."

I left quickly and forgot to talk with my aunt Carol, but I knew I would see her later. I knocked on the door, and Percy opened it up, and we gave each other the greatest hug ever known to man.

"Percy. I missed you, man. How are you doing?"

"Man. Life has been great! I learned a lot from being in the air force, and I saw the world. How are you doing? I missed the life out of you. Oh, wait. Look who I have with me."

I turned around and it was Katrina, eight months pregnant, and she showed me her wedding ring. I was wowed!

Percy continued, "Man! We live down in Atlanta. Come see us one day. I'm sorry, bro. How are you doing?"

I wished I could've told him the truth. That I needed him, but his life changed, and I couldn't bring him into my drama. If I told him the truth, he would have convinced me to move and change my life, or he would have made sure someone else would have taken care of what I needed. So instead of telling him the truth, I quickly changed the subject.

"Where's your pops?"

"He went out to grab some drinks to celebrate."

Katrina walked away from us, and I said to him,

"So, how long are the both of you back in town for?"

"We're here for around five days. We were coming to see her parents. We arrived in Brooklyn yesterday, and last night I saw one of my friends who always took care of me. He asked me to help him with a situation, and I couldn't refuse. You know how that goes."

I quietly nodded and said to myself that I should tell Percy now. But I didn't, and Katrina returned to her newlywed husband, and I told them I had to leave, and then we hugged each other.

"James. If you need help while I'm up here, call me ASAP."

I walked out of the apartment, and I went back to my grand-mother's house, but it had cops inside looking for me. Percy called me at the right time. But I didn't have any money, and I couldn't go back and hang with him and Katrina. I had to move on, but later that day I met a sexy-looking short blond-haired woman in another part of Brooklyn. I visited her the next two days, as she lived in another crime-infested neighborhood, and those dudes in that neighborhood weren't going to just let me be. I had to prove to them who I was and what I was about. I did that, but I knew on any given Sunday I could be throwing bullets back at them. I always had a feeling they wanted me dead. I was gaining too much love and too much attention from their ladies within two days! What was it that I did to be put on someone's hit list? Was it the—

"There he is, sir. Right there."

The supermarket security guard started walking over to me.

"Sir. You have been in this store for close to two hours and look like you're in trouble. I don't know what it is, but you're making the manager and some of the staff here nervous. They think you're trying to have this place set up for a robbery. Please buy your groceries or leave the store now."

He wasn't wrong, and I couldn't argue with him about it. I have to go. Let's get this over with. Let's get it on! I walked over to the cashier to pay for the items in my shopping cart, and there were two people in front of me. Ironically, any other time when I needed the line to move fast, it didn't, and now I'm ready to die, these people have a lot of groceries and the light is blinking red for the manager's assistance. Maybe self-consciously, I picked this line for more time to reflect, relax, and be rescued. Maybe I really needed this lane. After waiting for five minutes, I'm finally about to check out, and I see out the window three dudes and who the hell is that girl with them? It looks like—

"Excuse me, sir. Paper or plastic? Sir. Paper or plastic?"

I looked at her with my heart racing.

"Plastic, please."

"Your total is exactly fifty-six dollars, sir. Cash or credit?"

"Credit."

I paid, grabbed my bags, headed for the exit, and said to myself, Here we go! I started walking across and as soon as I got to the double yellow lines—

BANG! BANG!

I heard gunshots, then I heard some words. I hit the ground, and I see the dudes and that bitch running away. To my right, I think it was the dude who probably shot me bending over trying to catch his breath and a supermarket customer screaming,

"He's been shot! Someone shot him!"

I don't know where I was hit, but my back on my lower left side was killing me. I started thinking, Where's my friend? Was he down with this? I hear the police and ambulance sirens nearby, and it felt like a long time since I've been here. Then I heard, "Oh my God! Oh my God! This is my cousin James!"

I looked up, and it was Tiffany. All I did was smile because I knew she would save me. I closed my eyes.

III

Part Three

Laura

Once she pulled me by my hair, ran me against the door, threw me on the ground, stood over me, flicked her cigarette on my face. "If you're so damn smart then bring my husband back bitch."

<u>*Character List*</u>

Laura: *Main character/narrator*
Andre: *Laura's husband*
Tracy: *Laura's mother/Ricardo's wife*
Renee: *Tracy's sister*
Alex: *Laura's brother*
Ricardo: *Laura's father*
Barbara: *James's mother/Ricardo's mistress*
James: *Barbara's son*
Douglass: *Laura's cousin*
D Justice & **Double D**: *Friends*

Chapter Seven

"And I'd like to raise a toast. To a wonderful couple whom I have known for eight of their ten years of marriage, and to Laura and her wonderful career. Here's to your ten-year anniversary and your promotion to executive television producer."

"Thank you, Jan. We truly appreciate it. We love you. You know, these last ten years have been so amazing, and I...I'm sorry, our babysitter is calling me." I walked away and answered the call.

"Hello, Annie. What's going on?"

"Hello. Just wanted to tell you that there is a cop car sitting in front of the house now."

"How long has it been there?"

"Maybe ten minutes."

"Ok. We will be on our way."

My husband walked over to me. "Is everything fine, baby? What's wrong?"

"I'll tell you when we get in the car."

We walked over to everyone.

"We're sorry, everyone. Seems like we have a small emergency to tend to at home. Thank you, Jan, Thomas, Charles, and Marian for helping celebrate our tenth anniversary tonight. We will call everyone when we get home."

After we all exchanged hugs and kisses, we left. My husband and I jumped in our new Range Rover that I bought him for his birthday last year, and he started driving.

"What happened? Who was that on the phone? Why do you look so shaken?"

"Annie called and said there is a police car parked out in front of the house. She said they have been there almost ten minutes, and they never rang the bell or got out of the car."

"Well, maybe they are just taking a rest, doing paperwork, or watching the neighborhood. I'm going to play some jazz to relax us until we get there."

I looked at my wonderful husband. "Maybe you're right, baby."

I stared out the window, as we had at least an hour-and-a-half ride back.

I knew this day would come because I knew I couldn't escape this feeling forever. Every time I heard police sirens, I stood still and told myself that this was it and my life was over. But it either drove by me or stopped at another home in any neighborhood I lived in. I have a wonderful and educated husband and a wonderful marriage. It was love at first sight. We have three awesome daughters, ages nine, six, and four years old. We have a huge seven bedroom and six bathroom six thousand square foot home in one of the affluent neighborhoods in Connecticut. I was recently promoted to executive producer. I'm thirty-seven years old, and I have a decade-old secret, which is I conspired to commit murder.

I'm not an evil person. I never was, but I had to do what I had to do. It was justified because it was an eye for an eye, so I never was going to turn myself in. I was a good girl, but one moment changed my life. I had a great and wonderful childhood. My mother was a beautiful White woman from California who moved to New York City in the mid-seventies for a career in modeling. Over the next few years, my mother could not get any modeling jobs, and without any formal education, she applied for an assistant secretary position at a meat manufacturer where my father worked. As soon as they met, they instantly fell head over heels and quickly married.

I'm the oldest, and I'm three years older than my only brother, Alex. We had fun growing up. Anything we wanted we got and more. My father was a gorgeous tall Black man who was a single child and spoiled by his wealthy mother. He was an educated man who was calm, soft spoken, respectful, and embraced by everyone he met. We lived in the upper east side of Manhattan, and my brother and I went to the best private schools, had toys everywhere, and felt love every day. We adored our father, as he loved living life. There were two nights that changed my life, and tonight when we reach home will be my third night. The first night was when I was fourteen years old. I was in my room watching television around nine o'clock, and my aunt Renee came over and went directly to my mother. Shortly after she arrived, my mother screamed, "Why? Why? What did I ever do to him to deserve this? I love him too much, and he does this to me."

"He's been doing this for the last two years? Instead of traveling, he was spending time with her and her sons? That's why I saw them on Sunday in Manhattan. I thought they were his nephews, but they were acting as his kids. I'm sorry, girl, but you can't blame yourself or her. She probably had no idea what he was doing. He's wrong for this. Now what do you want to do?"

After I heard my mother and my aunt talking, my stomach was turning because I knew my father somehow messed up really badly, but I couldn't tell exactly what he did. I quickly thought about the times my father treated me as the only princess in the world. Just holding his hand while crossing the street or explaining life to me were remarkable moments being stolen from me.

Then my mother said, "I know that bitch. I knew she always wanted my husband, but he is a man. A good-looking, well-dressed, sexy, and educated man who just couldn't help himself with women throwing themselves at him. Out of all the women in the world, he got with her because the only thing she has over me is a fucking college degree. My love for him is unquestionable, but we can't stay together."

I thought about what my mother said about that woman having a college degree, and I remember the times when my mother's intelligence made my father feel very disappointed with her. My mother's parents were hippies, were never married, were poor, and they barely loved each other. My grandmother later married an educated man who downplayed her and left her for an educated woman, and my mother saw that and hated it. Therefore, I see why my mother felt how she did about the drama that unfolded in her lap. I felt ashamed for her, and I told myself those moments will not happen to me. My goal was to receive at least my master's degree and make my mother proud, but deep down inside I knew she would be disappointed with my achievements with it being a one-up on her kind of thing. My father loved the way I used my intelligence and expressed my goals to be successful. I wanted to go to the same university he did and definitely make him proud.

While my mother and aunt were still talking, my father came

through the door, and my mother ran to him. She started slapping him in the face over and over.

"You fucking bastard! You've been cheating on me and your family. You fucking bastard! I want you out of this house. You cheated on me with that smart bitch! You bastard!"

My father spoke in a calm, smooth voice,

"I love you, and I love her the same. The heart wants what it wants. Yes, I'm certainly the bastard you called me, but I will never stop falling in love with you. I'll pack my things and let you know where I'm staying."

After he packed two bags, he walked up to me and my brother.

"My beautiful girl and handsome little man. I messed up and will have to take some time away from home. Trust me when I say I never meant to hurt anyone, but I couldn't prevent falling in love with your mother and another woman. I will be nearby whenever any one of you needs me."

As we hugged him and cried, I looked up and saw my mother crying because she loved him, and she knew he was still in love with her. He let us go, went to grab some other things, and before he left, my mother said to him, "Ric, this is our home. Come back when you want to. We will work this out."

My father looked at her and was about to cry. "Yes. But I really need a break from my lifestyle, and you're right that I need to leave. I've been wrong for so long that I have to let all of us heal."

He left, and my mother cried and threw picture frames, table lamps, and anything she could grab across the living room. Over the next few weeks, we talked to him over the phone, but we never actually saw him again. From the moment my father Ricardo left, my mother and our relationship started to spiral.

One week after my father left, he did not call her, and she

became deranged. She would just snap and throw dishes and damage cabinets in the kitchen until she fell on the floor. For the first couple of weeks, she was convinced he was secretly with the other family. But after a month, she was told that he stopped coming to work, and that really pissed her off. She had a number of "spies" trying to find him and report to her about his whereabouts, but they couldn't find him. His phone was cut off, and none of us could reach him. He fell off the face of the earth. However, during the second month, she received word that he wasn't with the other family, and that news put her in a depression. By him staying with them, at least she could keep tabs on him and lure him back to her. She stopped eating and drinking like she used to, and she just stared at the walls and walked around like a zombie. It was bad because I had to cook meals for me, her, and Alex. In the third month, she stopped working, and so they fired her, but she would show up to see if he came to work. When he didn't come out, she caused a scene, falling down crying, hoping my father would receive word of what occurred so he would go home and attend to his wife's mental health.

One afternoon she brought us with her to stand outside waiting for him. One of the managers who knew us said,

"Hi, Tracy. Hello, Alex and Laura. Tracy, what's going on? Why are you here?"

She smirked at him.

"Hello, Tom. We're waiting for Ricardo so we can greet him. Is he coming out soon?"

He looked at us, looked up in the sky, and took a deep breath.

"Tracy. People told you two months ago that Ricardo quit. Different employees told me they told you this at least once a week. I guess this is my turn. He's not coming back. Please stop hurting yourself and the kids this way."

"Fuck you, dumb motherfucker! I know you're lying for him. He's at his desk with some dumb whore. Come on, kids, let's go. We'll be back tomorrow."

As we started walking away, I couldn't believe she knew he didn't work there anymore.

We were embarrassed to be with my mother. She kept going back, and we never did. My father resigned as soon as my parents separated, and she just couldn't take it. She stopped looking for years and just stayed in a depressed state. The years between fourteen and eighteen for me were pure hell. Alex was eleven years old when my mother started going off the deep end, and so he got lucky. Because he looked so much like my father, she got depressed every time she looked at Alex. To take away her pain, she sent him to military school until he turned eighteen, then he went to college. I wasn't that lucky or lucky at all. I have been physically and emotionally abused. She was cursing at me every day, especially when I brought home all A's because it reminded her of the man who wasn't coming back to her. When I showed her, she said, "So what? You think you're smarter than me? You little bitch."

Once she pulled me by my hair, ran me against the door, threw me on the ground, stood over me, and flicked her cigarette on my face. "If you're so damn smart, then bring my husband back, bitch."

When I was seventeen, I banged on her bathroom door because she was in the bathtub and the water was overflowing and dripping onto the room below. She answered the door and looked at me. "Ok. You think you're grown now, little bitch."

She grabbed my hair and pulled me to the top of the steps and threw me down, giving me a concussion, and screamed down,

"Bring him back, bitch!"

So that year I went to his old job and talked to his old secretaries, and one of them told me where he was staying. I was told that he just recently came back to check in. I went there one morning, but his neighbor told me he went to the Dominican Republic to be with his family. All I wanted was for him to come see my mother, but he wasn't there.

When I turned eighteen years old, after years of trying to get away from Tracy, I was accepted into Cornell University, and I spent four years away from her receiving my bachelor's in business. Because she was still in a depressed state over my father, she didn't come to graduation or told me congratulations because that would make me feel a little proud, and she would have accepted my one-up achievement. I was content with that. Instead of going back home and helping her, I got a job at a local news station as an associate producer. After a few years of being passed up for promotions because I didn't have a higher education, I left my position and enrolled into Georgia Southern University for my master's.

Then the heartbreaking news came when I received the call that my beloved father, the great and wonderful Ricardo Desire, was found dead in an apparent suicide, which also looked like a murder, and that pushed Tracy over the edge. I came back to Manhattan and stayed with Tracy, as did Alex, and we quickly realized she was definitely hurting. She kept all the lights off, looked like she didn't wash any dishes for years, with roaches running races for the dried and stuck meat and vegetables on plates, and she sure wasn't taking any daily regular showers or baths. All the years without him, she never recovered, but his death was a different kind of pain for all of us, especially Tracy.

Two days before my father's funeral, we were trying to

convince her to go to the funeral, and after hours of refusing to, she finally agreed to go. Then she told us good night and locked her bedroom door. The next morning we couldn't get her to answer the door, so we broke the door down and found her on her bed soaking in blood as she slit her wrists. So not only did both of my parents die within a week apart, but I became the lead person for both funerals. Her suicide note read,

I blame myself for not loving him the way he needed me to.

Chapter Eight

As I gazed out the passenger's side window looking at all the lights on the passing light poles, I was nervous as hell. Usually during my ten years of marriage to this great man, jazz normally calmed my mind and slowed down my heart rate, but not tonight. I look at this man and see nothing but love and strength. He saved me when I needed to be saved. And it started when I was twenty-seven, after my father and Tracy's funerals.

While I was at my father's funeral, I was a complete wreck. Both sides of my family knew of the news about my mother's suicide. Therefore, I had this funeral to deal with and my mother's the following week. The funeral home was jam-packed with a lot of family from the Dominican Republic and Haiti, also his friends and family. My father was a great and loved man. I sat in the front row close to the end of the hard wooden pews, and next to me at the very end was my cousin Douglass. He was twenty-five years old, and one of my cousins on my mother's side. He was White but was one of those White kids who grew up in a poor Black neighborhood in Brooklyn. He had to gain his respect to survive, so he knew very bad street people. However, Douglass had a rare kind of stomach cancer and was slowly dying.

While we were there talking, we started hearing people talking, and one of my father's closest secretaries yelled out, "There's that money-hungry homewrecker bitch!"

At the same time she was pointing toward the casket, Douglass and I looked up, and there they were, my father's mistress and her son. My father's mistress turned around and yelled, "I LOVED THIS MAN TOO. WE LOVED RICARDO. ALL OF Y'ALL JUST GO TO HELL!"

I looked at her and her son, and I said to myself that those two destroyed my life. They walked away, and Douglass and I looked at each other.

"L. I'm going to find where they live, and I promise you, we will catch them."

He got up, walked over to one of his street friends, and whispered in his ear. The friend walked out toward the main entrance, sort of like following the mistress and son.

After the burial, two detectives came up and confronted me and Alex.

"Ms. Desire, correct?"

"No. It's Ms. Parker."

"I apologize. I'm Homicide Detective Adam Singleton, and this is my partner Detective Steven Kinds. We're investigating the death of your father. Can we talk in private for a moment?"

"Sure."

We walked in front of the detectives toward our car, and Alex and I looked at each other.

"Listen Alex. Let me do all the talking. They probably will try to say that we killed Daddy."

"No problem. I'll just answer the simple questions if they ask me any."

We all stopped in front of the car, and Detective Adam

Singleton turned to us.

"We went to talk to your father's wife, but she hasn't been home the last few days."

"Well, my mother killed herself after hearing about my father's death. But I'm guessing you knew that already."

"We did. Can you think of anyone who would've wanted your father killed? The medical examiner confirmed that your father was murdered."

"I can't think of anyone who wanted my father dead. My mother loved that man. Yep. I can't think of anyone. Can you, Alex?"

"Everyone loved our father."

Then Detective Adam Singleton looked around.

"I'm sorry, but I have to ask, Ms. Parker. Where were you the morning your father was murdered?"

"I was in Georgia at graduate school."

"What about you, Mr. Parker?"

"I was also out of the state in college."

"Ms. Parker, you are the oldest, correct?"

"Yes, I am."

"Are you the primary beneficiary on both life insurances?"

"I am. However, I'm dividing it with my little brother."

"Thank you for your time, Mr. and Ms. Parker. We'll keep you both updated once we get more information or have any more questions."

A few weeks later, Douglass called me and wanted to meet up. We met around one o'clock on a hot Saturday in Prospect Park, and we waited for ten minutes before his friend Justice arrived with another guy and a girl. All three looked about my age, and all three were very dirty and grimy looking. Definitely not my kind of company or cups of tea. Douglass introduced everyone, and Justice said he was a friend of James, my father's mistress's son.

Douglass said, "Before we start, L, give me five dollars."

I looked at him funny because first why five dollars, and second, that meant I would have to take my wallet out and take out a five-dollar bill, which I also had a few twenties and fifties in it. I didn't want those people knowing what I had. I did all of that and gave him the five dollars, and he quickly handed it to Justice and said to him, "Now, this is a done deal."

Justice gave Douglass a piece of paper with James's mother's addresses on it.

I looked at the girl. "Can we talk privately?"

She nodded her head, and we started walking away from the guys. After walking, we sat a few benches away from them, and I took a deep breath. I just wanted to know who she was and her reasons. I just wanted to talk to her woman to woman.

"What's your name, and how do you know Douglass and Justice exactly?"

I never dealt with these kinds of people before, and I didn't know the rules of this game. Although I interviewed people for case studies as a graduate student, those were students with scenarios reading from index cards. I sure wasn't giving her my name or the purpose of knowing James because she didn't need to know. I'm not from the streets, but I'm not a dummy either.

She looked at me.

"You can call me Double D, and I don't know Justice. I don't know the other guy, Douglass, either. I never saw those guys in my life, but the other guy is my close friend Daniel. We go back to elementary school. We grew up together on the same block as James."

"Wow. So how well do you know James? What type of guy is

he?"

"I had a crush on James since elementary school, but I never told him my feelings, hoping that he would come to me first. I was planning on him being my first. I loved the way he moved and his smile, but he had some major drama in his life. We all did. We all went to the same high school, and he introduced me to his friend, who did me wrong, and I wasn't happy with James about that. It changed my life, as I went into a tailspin. This is why I look like this. I have followed him every day since that day so I know where he and his children's mothers live. I even know the psychiatric ward his mother lives at."

She kept talking, and I sat there just thinking how our lives are very different but could have been the very same. I could have easily gone down the road she was on, especially since my father left and I didn't have a strong male in my life. But my father taught me the right way to have a man treat me. She had a strong father who chased her drug addict mother around until they both died. She was living with her grandmother trying to keep it together until that guy came along and ruined her life. I, on the other hand, was twenty-seven years old, and the first boyfriend I had was during my first year in college when I was eighteen years old. He was an asshole, and he wasn't going to be my first, so I was still waiting for Mr. Right. I had no idea what I was going to do with my father's mistress or her son because I wasn't street savvy, but I wanted them to feel what I felt. It seems like they might have felt that feeling already.

BING! BING! BING! BING! BING!

"Laura. Laura. *Laura*! Baby, your phone is going off with text messages."

I looked at my husband, then down at my phone, and the same message was popping up from our babysitter. I looked at my husband.

"Baby, the cop car is still there in front of the house."

I texted her back that we will be there soon and we were only forty minutes away.

"Baby. I'm so happy to be your wife. You've always been there when I needed someone."

"I love you, Laura. You stole my heart."

I looked back out the window, and I kept thinking about that girl Double D.

We walked back to the guys, and Douglass said, "So, let me talk to my cousin, and we'll reach out to everyone again."

We all said goodbyes, and Douglass and I walked away and started talking.

"Look, L. What's the end goal here?"

"I feel like I need them to hurt more than I did, but after talking to Double D, I feel I need to do some soul searching and forgiveness. But his mother's actions did hurt my family."

"Whatever you want to do, I got you. But those motherfuckers don't give a shit about you or our family. Take this paper and go visit your pop's mistress. Spend some time with her. Pick her brain, and see what you get."

I had no choice but to go along with his plans. The next day I went to the hospital, walked up to the front desk, and signed in as L. P.

The receptionist said, "Hello. How can I help you?"

"I am here to speak with Mrs. Barbara Smith."

Wow! Looking back at that time, it was the first time I spoke her name. Even now I can't believe I remembered her name. Near the front desk was an open area where around ten residents were watching television and spending time away from their rooms.

The receptionist looked straight at me.

"And who are you?"

"I'm her niece."

After looking down into the registered visitors' book, she looked back up at me.

"Mrs. Smith has only four authorized visitors, and darling, with your pretty face and your fancy clothes, you are not one of them. You have to leave."

"Please. Please. It is extremely important that I speak to her."

"You cannot talk to her without being authorized to do so."

I turned around and took three steps toward the exit.

"Stop, pretty girl. Let me walk over and ask Mrs. Smith if she wants company. She hasn't had a visitor in a good time now."

She walked to one of the residents and touched the back of the chair that was facing me.

"Mrs. Barbara. There's a different visitor for you. It's your niece."

Mrs. Smith looked up at the receptionist.

"I don't care if it was the pope, tell them to leave me the fuck alone."

The receptionist turned her around to see me, and before the receptionist said a word,

"I don't know that bitch! She probably came to kill me."

The receptionist turned her back around and walked toward me.

"I apologize for that, but you have to go now. Sorry, pretty lady."

It was on from that moment. Mrs. Smith made my decision for me. I walked out and called Douglass and told him what happened. I told him that there is no way he could touch Mrs. Smith. Therefore, to hurt her like I was hurt, Douglass and

Justice had to focus on James.

Douglass had eyes on James's every move, and he was just waiting when the time was right. He called me and told me that he found out that James was staying with one of his girlfriends in Brooklyn. Douglass said, "Laura. We got him. I told Justice, and he and Double D agreed to meet us there wherever and whenever. She wants to see his face when we take him down."

I didn't care if she was there, but we had to do this soon. I was on summer break, and I had to go back. I told Douglass, "Let's do it a week from now." Douglass told Justice, and he was going to let us know the time and place. Then all of a sudden Douglass died of his stomach cancer, and now with a day to go back to school, I had to deal with Justice. He called me.

"Baby girl. I will take care of this. Do what you have to do, and don't look back. Douglass gave me your number when he went into the hospital the other day."

"Thank you. What about Double D?"

"I'm not telling her anything, but my man D will come along and watch in the background. Take care and don't look back."

The next day around three o'clock, I got on a plane, and I never looked back. I didn't even go to Douglass's funeral, but I sent a lot of flowers.

Chapter Nine

On that day, I felt horrible, but it also became one of the greatest days of my life. I shouldn't have even been in Brooklyn that day because I was scheduled to go back to school the week before my break was over. I had to set up an event for my professor because I was her assistant during my last semester of graduate school. But the revenge spell overcame me; therefore, I lied to my professor, telling her I needed another week to help with Douglass's funeral. The day James was killed, I should've been back on campus. However, because I was in Brooklyn that day, I had to get on a plane instead of taking the Amtrak. Because I paid for the flight last minute, I had to wait for a standby seat, and no one wanted to give up their seat. I stood there mad as hell, and then it happened. Someone missed their flight, and I got the last seat. I didn't know it at the time, but the seat was the middle seat, and my future husband was sitting in the aisle seat.

"Excuse me, sir. I'm in the middle seat."

He looked up at me.

"This is my lucky day."

In my mind, I was screaming for joy because he was so attractive. Then I thought in my mind but it came out,

"This is my lucky day too."

He looked at me, and we smiled at each other. I sat down, and before the flight instructions came on the speaker, we officially exchanged greetings. His name was Andre, and inside my head I was so excited. I couldn't believe that this good-looking man was finding me interesting. Once we took off, we quietly were talking to each other.

"So, Andre. Are you from New York? What part? I'm from the upper east side of Manhattan."

"Yes. I'm from Brooklyn. Born and raised."

"So where are you heading to?"

"I'm heading back to school. I attend Georgia Southern University."

I was so freaking shocked.

"I go to Georgia Southern!"

"Get out of here. I'm in my final semester of getting my bachelor's in criminal justice."

I fell in love with him as soon as he said that.

"Wow. Well, Andre, I'm in my last semester in grad school studying television production. I love criminal justice."

"Wow! We're going to work very well together. What were you doing in New York during the summer break?"

"Well, I had to attend to some family business. What about you?"

Right before he answered, I saw his body language, and it was as if he really didn't want to talk about his family, and I definitely understood that.

"Just seeing family, which I'm really beginning not to do anymore."

I quickly changed the subject.

"Criminal justice. I can't ever marry you because you would

try to handcuff me to you for life."

I don't know why I said that, but I think it was because of the vibe he was giving me.

He smiled.

"So far I think I'll like that."

We talked the whole flight through, and being with him, I couldn't remember the crime I was involved in hours before. Even to this day, he makes me forget about everything except for love and family. Maybe I was falling for the wrong guy, but my gut and heart told me he was the right guy. After the plane landed, when we walked off together, I just knew the cops were waiting at the gate standing there to take me back to Brooklyn, but they weren't. I kept walking with my future husband, and we shared a taxi to school.

He stared at me.

"I like the time we shared, and I want you in my life. Can I take you out for lunch and dinner sometimes?"

"Let's do breakfast every morning after we do dinners every night."

We agreed, exited the taxi, said our goodbyes, then I walked away thinking he was an undercover cop and I was just set up. But I made it to my room safely. Soon after we both graduated that December, we found jobs, got married, and started a family. Years later we moved to Connecticut.

Now, looking out the car window and back at him, I'm saying to myself how in the hell I'm going to tell him that the cops are waiting for me. He's an eight-year veteran homicide detective, and this will destroy him mentally and career-wise. How is he supposed to catch murderers when one has been living under his own roof for ten years? Sleeping in his bed and keeping him warm every night? This wonderful man has been very supportive and just a blessing in my life, and I'm going to ruin him. Every time I hear a cop car, I just know it is my last day of freedom. Ironically, this man doesn't even know the woman he's been protecting. They will probably try to connect him with my crime and say he was harboring a fugitive and wouldn't even care if the truth was far from their accusations. However, if he knew, he would have protected me. I adore this man, and we are a block away from the house.

I have to tell him. But who told on me? Who connected the dots and found me living in Connecticut? Could it have been Justice? Although he had my phone number and name, the way he proclaimed his love for loyalty, I couldn't see him telling the police a story to save his own skin. However, I didn't know him that well, and I heard from one of my other cousins when I was at my aunt's funeral last year who was Douglass's half brother, Ben, that Justice was killed five years ago in a shoot-out. Is that how they found me? Did Douglass tell Ben what I was doing with Douglass, and Ben gave me up? Why else would he tell me out of the blue that Justice died? Now that I think of it, I kind of got the vibe like my secret was safe with him.

Could it have been Double D? Ironically, she also was at my aunt's funeral. She looked cleaned up but still not what she should and could have. We spoke, as she was dating Ben. She gave me that look as if she didn't like what went down with James. Then I walked to her and gave her a hug. I looked in her eyes, and before I said anything, I heard, "Ever since James was killed, I haven't been able to sleep. We should have never done that."

I thought, We shouldn't have done that? Is she trying to set me up? Maybe at the time I was paranoid or too much into solving crimes thinking like my husband. Nonetheless,

I learned that once you are in the game, trust no one.

We turned the corner and were now on our block, and we saw the cop car in front of our home.

"Darling, pull over for a second. I have to tell you something."

He pulled over and had a fearful look, but with a we can overcome this sound in his voice.

"What is it, baby?"

"Look, baby. I have to tell you something I have been holding in for too long."

"Laura. If there's another man in your life, why didn't you talk to me about it? I believe I have been the best husband any woman could ask for and need in life. You could've come to me about this. Is it someone at the television station?"

I had my head down, facing my lap, quietly crying because I never meant for him to ever have had that thought in his mind. He was hurt. I turned to him, wiping my tears.

"Of course not. It's nothing like that. I held a secret from you for the ten years we been married, actually from the first day. When we first met, I knew we were meant to be in each other's lives. That was one of the best days in my life, and it was also one of the worst days in my life. Hours before we met, I was part of a crime—actually, I was part of a murder. During that summer, my father was murdered in his home. The crime scene looked like a suicide, but my father would have never taken his life, but he did fall into a depressed state years before. Then my mother actually committed suicide because she believed his death was on her. I always told you, the girls, and our family and friends that my parents died when I was young, and they did, but when I was an adult. I tried to block them from my mind and keep moving. I had to bury both of them a week apart. When we get to the house and get out of the car, I will be arrested, and I wanted to tell you the secret I have been holding because you deserve the truth, and I never meant to hurt you or the girls. Just please continue to protect them when I'm gone."

"Wow! How could this be? Does anyone else know? Who can connect you to the crime? Listen to me, Laura. This is extremely important. Who knows about you and this crime?"

"Of the four of them, two died, and the other two I think are still living, but I don't believe they know my last name."

"Do you know the whereabouts of these people? I know a few detectives who could assist with helping us find them."

"I don't know because my cousin did all the dirty work."

"Call the babysitter and tell her that we're going back into the city. I will call my people at the station and tell them to recall the unit that is in front of the house, and the girls will be fine. We'll go see the two people who know about this."

As I sat there sobbing and wiping my face, I thought to myself that this man is going to protect me by any means necessary. He's been doing that for more than ten years, and I couldn't let him do that anymore. We both can't get caught up in this mess. The girls will definitely need one of us to navigate them through this life, which can actually change swiftly.

"No. We are not doing that. I am tired of running and having the feeling of being scared. Let's go home and take on what comes next."

"It's your choice, and I'm supporting you as I always have. But the media will probably have a field day with our daughters knowing I'm a detective and you're a television producer for the investigation network."

"I know, but let's get this over with. And I will always love you. I have loved you since I sat next to you on the plane."

"I love you so much. And nothing will ever change that. Let's do this!"

He slowly drove up to the house, and I wanted to get this moment over with. As soon as he stopped behind the cop car, I jumped out and walked quickly to the cop car, and there was an undercover cop car down the block, and two detectives got out and started walking toward us. In total, there were two tall White male Connecticut police officers and two New York City detectives. One was a Black male and the other a Black female who swiftly walked up to us. I walked up, and before I said anything, my husband slammed his car door and stood by my side. "Officers. Here I am! I'm ready, but please don't do this in front of my house. My daughters are looking out the windows."

The woman detective looked at me.

"Mrs. Brown. My name is Detective Olena Jackson, and this is Detective Donnie Whitehead."

"Look, Detective Jackson. I'm ready."

"Ready for what?"

"Detective, why are you here?"

"We are here for him, to arrest your husband."

She walked to Andre, turned my husband around, and placed handcuffs on him.

"Detective Andre Brown. You are under arrest for the murder of Ricardo Desire."

Chapter Ten

What the hell? They turned him back around facing me. I looked in his eyes, and he looked in my eyes, and I couldn't believe what he had done. Who was this man I married? I thought I knew who he was. I looked at my daughters as all of them ran out the front door holding on to their father screaming, "Daddy! This is our daddy. Let my daddy go!"

He looked down at them. "Don't worry about me, girls. I'll be home soon. This is just a mistake. Laura, call our lawyer."

"I will."

But I was shocked. How did I marry the man who possibly killed my beloved father? How did he know my father? Did he kill my father and marry me as payback? Maybe setting me up to also kill me? I started thinking about the questions the detectives on the shows I produced would ask. Do I still love this man even though he possibly killed my father? I had to find out who this man was. This meant as I confessed my crime to Andre, he was also a criminal on the run. Do I fight for my husband and continue to live in a so-called wonderful marriage? I love him, and I hate him. My emotions are everywhere. If I don't help him, I'll be seen as a woman who just gave up on her husband, and people will understand, but it will look suspicious. If I do help him, I'm the beloved wife who protected her husband even though he killed her father. It would look like he and I worked together to collect my father's money. However, for the sake of my daughters, I have to support him. I couldn't believe that my life could end up like one of the hundreds of stories I produced over my career.

I have to find out who my husband was and how he committed the crime. I thought I could ask the hundreds of detectives I met over the years, but I feared I would be exposed. I thought of hiring a private investigator. I took my daughters inside the house, calmed them down, called our lawyer, Kimberly Jacobson, and she picked up immediately.

"Kim. It's Laura Brown. Andre has been arrested and is being taken to Central Bookings in Brooklyn for murder."

"Hello, Laura. Ok, I'll come get you in the morning, and we will head down to New York, since he should be arraigned in the morning. Because he's a detective, they will protect him and place him in his own jail cell. I will call you in the morning."

The next morning Kim called and came to my house.

"So, Laura. Before we head to New York, I need to know what you know."

"Kim. All I know is that he was arrested for murdering a man named Ricardo Desire ten years ago before we met each other."

I couldn't tell her Ricardo was my father because that could potentially connect me to James's murder.

"Don't worry, Laura. I'll reach out to one of my investigators to look into this. Let's get going."

We drove to the courthouse in Brooklyn, and we sat and waited an hour for his case to be called. Then his case was called, he came out, and Kim went up to him.

The judge said, "How do you plea, Detective Andre Brown?"

"Not guilty, Your Honor."

Kim jumped in. "Your Honor. My client is a veteran of the Hartford, Connecticut, homicide unit and is highly respected and highly decorated—"

She was interrupted by the prosecutor.

"Your Honor. The suspect Detective Andre Brown should not make bail because of his heinous crime of murdering Ricardo Desire ten years ago. Also because of his political and financial connections."

The judge nodded. "Yes. I remember that murder. It came in front of me during my first year on the bench. Bail denied."

Kim and I walked out of the courtroom.

"Political and financial connections? What the hell is that prosecutor talking about? Andre doesn't have any connections! I make way more money than he does."

"Laura. We will find out. Also, I'll talk to my investigator, and she will get right on the case. Do you know anything about Andre's past? I need to give her a head start."

"Andre never wanted to talk about his past or family. Every time he went to Brooklyn, he went by himself. He hated going to New York, especially Brooklyn. He definitely didn't want me to know, and I did the same, as I was running from my family."

"What are his parents' names? Siblings?"

"Kim, I don't know."

"You've been married for ten years, and you don't know anything? We're going to have to talk with Andre tomorrow at Rikers Island."

She drove me home, and I still couldn't wrap my head around who Andre really was.

The next day Kim and I met up and drove to Rikers Island, which is a horrible place to visit. I saw all these women and children being body searched and fighting for their men to come home. How many of these women are fighting the good fight for men who are totally innocent? We finally sat down, and Andre arrived. We kissed each other.

"Laura, baby. I'm so sorry I put you in this position. I hate putting you in a place where you have to visit me every week."

"Andre, honey. How are you holding up?"

Before he could say anything, Kim asked,

"Andre. Who are you? Better yet, who were you? Did you do this crime? Can you think of something that can connect you to this crime?"

"I did this when I was twenty-four years old. No one could possibly know what I did. There weren't any witnesses, and it happened so fast. But I'm not going to fight this anymore."

I was stunned. As a matter of fact, I don't think stunned is the correct word for what I was feeling. He killed my father! And I'm protecting the man who admitted killing him. Why? Because of love? He's the reason I'm in this mess. I have to know.

As Andre and I held hands, Kim looked at us.

"Look. You know the judge will not take your plea without the whole story. Let me help you before you plead guilty. Don't do this. Give me your background and a lead."

Andre looked unmoved by Kim's speech.

"Look, baby? We need to know how you knew that man and why you killed him. Also, what political and financial ties do we have that I don't know about?"

"I can't tell you anymore. Guard! I'm ready to go back. I love you, Laura, and please kiss the girls for me."

He stood up, and we kissed, then Kim stood up.

"Andre. Give me your mother's, brother's, or a friend's

name.”

"I can't. Just let me be.”

Kim and I left Rikers Island and started driving back.

"We're going to have to find who Ricardo Desire was. If we find that answer, then we can connect the dots.”

As soon as we got off the bridge, I knew I had to tell Kim who Ricardo Desire was before this case got deeper. I already lied to her that I didn't know him, but the truth will come out and I will look like a suspect. I wasn't in New York the time of his death; however, if my involvement with James's murder comes out, who's to say I couldn't set up my beloved father to be killed?

"Kim, I have to tell you something. Ricardo Desire was my father.”

She slammed on the brakes, pulled over on the side, and we jumped out of her car.

"What the hell, Laura? How could that be? What are the odds that could happen? Do you think Andre knew that?”

"There isn't any chance we knew each other. We met by chance on a flight to Georgia. Please don't tell him. It would break his heart to know this.”

"Laura! This is not good. If he knows, he will probably open up and tell the truth. I'll tell you what, if we can't get to the bottom of this, I'm telling my client.”

"Your client? I'm paying you. I'm your client too, correct?”

"I love you like a sister, and you are paying me, but he's my client, not you, Laura. Of course, there is husband and wife privilege, but that goes out the window if you knew or assisted in the crime. Did you?”

"Of course I didn't.”

We got back into her car and drove off. I thought his history would expose my history.

"Let's see what the ADA has."

Damn. I knew these two lawyers would definitely connect the dots. She pulled over and called ADA Joseph Becks, and with my luck, he picked up the phone.

"ADA Becks? This is Kim Jacobson from the Jacobson Law Firm. I need to see you. Oh, today is great. I can be there in twenty minutes. Thanks."

Kim joyfully looked at me.

"Laura. We're going to find out what the ADA knows."

We reached ADA Becks's office, and after we introduced ourselves, he and his assistant welcomed us to sit around an old white wooden table. Then ADA Becks stated,

"Well, there isn't any other way to put this, but your client will either get the death penalty or life without parole. He's not going to walk. Now, what can I help you with?"

"Tell us how you came to arrest a decorated detective like Andre Brown?" Kim asked.

"We have Detective Brown at the scene of the crime, and someone who knows him signed an affidavit and will testify Detective Brown committed the murder."

"Well, I have to know about this only witness. What's the name?"

"His name is Daniel Scott. He goes by the street name of D."

Oh shit! Is this the same D who knows me and can connect me to James? I played it cool and said to ADA Becks,

"So you're telling us that the man I was married to for ten years, the most faithful and honest man in my life, a man who never hurt a suspect even when they were the worst killers on this earth—you are telling us that some guy named D is your only witness? Let's talk to this D guy."

"Yes. We need to talk with Mr. Daniel Scott." Kim stated.

"You can only talk to him one time because he's currently in witness protection."

"Witness protection? For what?" I asked.

"Because of your husband's political and financial ties."

"Political and financial ties? You have the wrong man. You should drop the charge and let him free."

"Mrs. Brown. Do you know your husband? I don't think you do. Your husband has strong ties to people who can have others jailed or killed almost anywhere in the world. Now, I'm definitely not going to tell you who they are, but I suggest you ask him and do your homework before trial."

I stood up, stormed out of his office, and I waited for Kim.

"Kim. Use that investigator of yours and get everything we need to know."

I left the building, and I planned on visiting Andre the next day.

The next day I went through the whole degrading process of seeing my husband on Rikers Island. As I stood there, I asked myself, Who in the hell is this man? Do I still believe in him?

Soon he arrived and he sat down. We reached over the table and kissed.

"Andre, who are you?"

"I'm a man who made one huge mistake, but I knew what I was doing. The less you know, the better. Like you said, the girls can't lose both parents in this cruel and cold world."

"Fine. Tell me about the political and financial ties you have?"

"I don't know what they are talking about. I swear, Laura. I don't know."

"It's fine, baby. Do you know Daniel Scott, or a man named D?"

He looked puzzled.

"Yeah. Why?"

"He's the person who's testifying against you. He's the link between you and Ricardo Desire's murder."

BANG!

He banged the table.

"What? Find out where we can reach him."

"I can't because he's in witness protection."

"Don't worry. He's a former crack addict. We will beat this case. But let me ask you something. Do you know D?"

He looked into my eyes, trying to find my answer by looking into my soul. I think he suspected that I knew Daniel Scott. Maybe it's because of the way I asked him about Daniel, but there was a creepy feeling to his question.

"Hell no. Why would you ask me that?"

"I'm sorry. It's just my detective's way of thinking. Please, baby, don't take it personally."

"Andre. Kim and I believe there's a lot missing from your story. What's going on?"

"What, you don't believe me? Just run with it, and when the time is right, I will tell you everything. The less you know, the better."

We stood up, kissed, and the guard started walking him away, but the feeling I was getting from Andre was an untrustworthy vibe. I had a feeling he knew more than he was letting on, so I had to treat my husband with extreme caution.

Chapter Eleven

The next day while I was at home Kim called me.

"Good morning, Laura. ADA Becks set up a meeting between him, us, and Mr. Daniel Scott tomorrow afternoon at his office over the phone."

"Sounds great. Please come pick me up tomorrow morning."

I hung up the phone, and I spent that entire day wondering what Daniel would say. I was on pins and needles, and I didn't sleep that night. The next day we arrived at ADA Becks's office, and they called Daniel.

Kim said, "Mr. Scott."

Daniel responded with a deep and raspy voice. "Yeah?"

"Good afternoon. I'm Kimberly Jacobson from the Jacobson Law Firm. As you know, you are on a conference call with ADA Joseph Becks, his assistant ADA Kathy Jones, my client's wife, and me. How are you doing? We would like to hear your story."

"My story is the same I told Mr. Becks and Detective Jackson. I know your client, and I know he was the one who killed Mr. Ricardo."

"How can you be so sure? Did you see the crime? Did you see the actual crime scene? Did he tell you anything about it? Were you there?"

"Nah. I didn't see it, and he didn't tell me any of that. But I know."

"Sir. What kind of deal are you getting for your testimony?"

"Listen. I'm not in any legal trouble. I just couldn't keep living with myself knowing this dude killed Mr. Ricardo. Look, I'm done answering these questions. I have dirt on all different kinds of people. Shit. Get me one of those future 'get out of jail free' cards, and I can produce some names."

Right there I secretly signaled to Kim to end the call because I didn't need him to start talking, making deals, and spitting out names.

"Thank you for your cooperation, Mr. Scott." Kim stated.

The call ended, and Kim said to ADA Becks, "I don't believe his story or if it will hold any weight in court. Good luck with that witness. We'll see you in court."

We left, and the next day we returned to Rikers Island.

Kim said to Andre,

"Andre. If you still want to be a free man, tell us what we're missing with this story. Yours and Mr. Scott's stories are not adding up. As a matter of fact, basically there is no story. He's not doing this for a lesser sentence. He never even committed a crime that he was arrested for, and he's doing this out of the kindness of his heart. He thinks he has you by the short and curlies. Why?"

"There is no way he can prove I was there. You know what, let's go to trial. I'm going to beat this."

We all got up to leave. I looked Andre in his eyes and kissed him on his lips.

Andre's trial date was months away. During that time, I went back to work, where I heard 'We are sorry to hear about this' and 'We can't believe this is happening to both of you' lines. I stopped visiting Andre because first, I had to continue working since my job wasn't giving me any sick leave or FMLA for "spouses in jail visit" time off. If Andre was going to prison or coming home, I still had to continue going to work. Second, I was so tired from driving back and forth to Rikers Island. The whole jail process is not for everyone. It takes a huge toll on everyone who is directly involved, especially paying lawyer fees. Sometimes I just wanted to quit or just die, but my daughters needed me.

I was so tired. Financially, we had to continue paying Kim and her investigator, and Andre wasn't giving them any new information, and that meant we were paying for them to just sit on their asses hoping to find something. I was at the point where all I wanted to know was if I could be connected and exposed for James's murder. And the only person who could do that was Double D. All I kept hearing in the back of my head was Andre's voice saying the less I know, the better. I decided that morning to just focus on our girls and work. I called Kim,

"Good morning, Kim. I can't keep paying you and your investigator, and since Andre is not cooperating, please stop using your investigator for this case. Unless we find new information from Andre's mouth, please keep me out of the loop."

"I understand about the money, but what if I can cut the cost a bit lower?"

"I can't. Please, Kim. All I want to know is if my husband finally speaks. Thank you."

One day I was at work and a detective who knew Andre walked up to me and started small talk. I worked with this detective before as an expert on an episode I was producing.

"Laura. I heard what happened. Let me know if there is

anything I can help with."

"We definitely appreciate that."

"Ok. I won't keep you. Tell him that we will see each other again."

As he was slowly walking away,

"Detective. You know what? We need to find an investigator."

"No problem. Look, here are three names. Two who work in Connecticut and one in New York."

"We really need this. Thank you."

My goal was to find the cheapest one that I could afford with a lot on their plate so they wouldn't have extra time to sneak around looking for extra stuff. I just needed one to find Double D's location. The two in Connecticut were expensive, especially since they would have to travel to New York a lot. I visited the one from New York at his office in Manhattan, and he told me that he would do everything in his power to find anyone and anything on earth for my case. I knew first, he was going to charge the hell out of me, and second, he would find more than what I needed him to. I told him no thank you, and I left his office.

I rode the elevator down to the lobby, and as I was looking down at my text messages, I bumped into this sloppy-looking thin White woman who also was looking down at her phone. I apologized, and so did she, and I looked her in her face.

"I was looking at my text messages, and I was about to search for a private investigator. The one I just interviewed with wasn't the right kind of person for me."

"Oh. This must be your lucky day because you just bumped into another one. My name is Sarah Mitchell. If you have time, we can talk, and you can decide if I'm the right investigator for you. Let's go to my office on the second floor."

"Sounds great."

I knew this was fate for me to meet her. I wanted to get to know her and hope I wasn't wasting my time. I stared at her and starting slowly smiling.

"Better yet, let's go across the street to a restaurant and have brunch. We can get comfortable and get to know each other."

We walked into the restaurant, sat down, looked at the menus, and then we ordered.

"Sarah. Tell me about yourself. Sell me on what you can bring to the table to help me."

"Well, I'm thirty-two years old and from Queens. I have two young daughters, ages four and six, and they keep me busy, but not too much to interfere with my work, of course. Unfortunately, I'm divorced, and since I made more money than he did, I'm paying him alimony and for his legal bills. We just weren't a good fit, and it's sad that it took us seven years to figure that out. That is how I got into this business. He was cheating on me, and I busted them together. It was a hard and long journey, but I knew when it was finalized, I wanted to help others who were in the same position I am in. I don't want people feeling and going through what I have. So here I am two years in."

As she sat there talking, I knew deep down inside it was fate. She was perfect! Too busy with her kids, debt, and personal anger, she will just do exactly what I needed. Only focusing on business, and none of that "going the extra mile for the client" crap. I felt comfortable with her.

"Now, tell me your story. What can I do for you?"

"I'm just looking for a woman around thirtysomething, Black and probably a drug addict, or at least recovering. I think she still lives in Brooklyn, but if not, still in New York. I need to know her whereabouts, and I need to talk with her."

"What's her name?"

"I don't know her last name, but in the streets, she goes by Double D."

"Double D? Because of her breast size?"

"No. She was an A-cup when I last interacted with her. I need to talk to her."

"With a name like that, I can find her. Let's go back to my office and draw up the paperwork."

We walked back across the street and went inside her messy office. Her small office had paperwork everywhere, and I believed there were open cases. There were newspapers on the floor and on the chairs, empty cans of no-name supermarket sodas, and to top it off, overdue bills on her desk. Her ex-husband really screwed her over big time, and yep, I found the right one.

"I'm sorry for the mess. Please have a seat. Just throw those newspapers on the floor."

After clearing the seat, I sat down, and we talked about the cost, which was one flat fee up-front, and we talked about her process. The only question that I had was how this thin White woman was going to find Double D in the hood. But that's what I was paying her for.

A week before the trial Kim called me.

"Laura. Let's meet up and talk with Andre so we all know how the process will go."

She picked me up the next morning, and we headed to Rikers Island. We met with Andre, and he and I hugged, kissed, and exchanged greetings and Kim explained to us what would happen next. It felt crazy because he used to be on the stand during court cases and I produced and edited courtroom cases.

It was all coming full circle now. There were nights where Andre and I cuddled up on the couch watching television crime dramas and law shows guessing who the criminal was and the motive behind the crime, and during all that time, we both were secretly the real criminals, and both on the opposite side of the law.

"With no change in this case, it doesn't seem like freedom is in the air for us. But I have seen miraculous outcomes happen before. The first day the leading detective from the case and the medical examiner will both take the stand. The second day will be a character day. Ricardo's sister-in-law will take the stand for the state, and we have Andre's captain for us, and then you, Laura. The third day Mr. Daniel Scott will take the stand, then the fourth day Andre will take the stand. Our jury is made up of six men and six women, and hopefully they see it our way."

We got up, I hugged and kissed my husband who was making us broke goodbye. While we were walking, Kim stared at me.

"Laura. How are you holding up? How are those beautiful girls? When you take the stand, ADA Becks is going to try to catch you in a lie, so just be honest. And remember, you can call me anytime with any questions."

I knew that meant billable hours, and I wasn't falling for that. In our careers, Andre and I worked against and for lawyers, so I know billable hours when I see them. One word of information leads to questions, leads to "Let me find out," leads to "Here's your bill." Don't get me wrong, we loved Kim. We have known her for years, having dinners together, attending parties, and even sometimes celebrating holidays, but business is business, and she works for money, not hugs, kisses, and love. We drove back silently to Connecticut, and a block away from my home, my phone rang, and it was Sarah.

"Kim. Please stop the car. I can walk from here. I have to take this call."

She gave me this strange look like "What the hell are you hiding?"

"Ok, Laura. I will see you in a couple of days."

I got out of her car and answered the call. "Hello, Sarah. Any news on Double D?"

"Yes, indeed. Ms. Diane Downs, known as Double D, killed herself five years ago. She was living with her boyfriend, who was kind enough to let me into his apartment. However, he started acting weird when I told him I wasn't a cop, and that was strange because he has a long criminal record. I felt like he wished I was a cop. Nonetheless, he let me take a picture of her suicide note that I'm sending you now. I know this ends our business together, but please spread the word about my professionalism and work."

"Sarah. I will tell the world from the mountaintop. Thanks a million."

I walked into my house, sat down, and read the suicide note. It read,

Baby. I'm taking my life away from you and the boys. I can't continue to live with what I did. I'm so sorry that I turned out the way I did. Please take care of the boys. Hopefully I will see y'all in heaven.

I screamed for joy. I was so glad that she was gone. Only Daniel could connect me to James, and he barely could do that. His testimony probably wouldn't be admissible in court, straight secondhand testimony. And if she told her boyfriend, he would have told Sarah and not the cops. I loved it. I was ready to go to court.

Monday morning came, and Kim picked up me and my oldest

daughter, Jane, from our home to go to court. It was the first time any of our daughters had seen Andre since the day he was arrested. This long road was coming to an end, but my other dilemma came back to me. Do I want my wonderful husband of ten years who killed my beloved father found guilty? If that happened, that would destroy our family and put us in deeper financial debt. Or do I want him to be found innocent, restore order in our family, catch up on bills, start paying our debt, and be seen as a victim of the same justice system he worked for? Could I live with him knowing he killed my father for the rest of our lives? We stood in the row behind Kim and Andre, and he looked at us and smiled. We remained standing as the bailiff introduced Judge Aaron Stone, then we sat down.

"Good morning, everyone. Please place your phones on vibrate or off. I understand that we live in a cell phone–ruled world and information needs to be given quickly, but I will not allow ringing, alert sounds, or videotaping in my courtroom. Please have them on vibrate or off by the time we start every morning. Anyone who violates this rule will not be allowed to continue sitting in this courtroom during this trial. Now, both parties will state your names for the record during your opening remarks. But first, ladies and gentlemen of the jury. Today is the first day of the State of New York versus Andre Brown. Please keep a clear mind and pay close attention. ADA Becks, you have the floor."

"Thank you, Your Honor. Ladies and gentlemen of the jury. My name is ADA Joseph Becks, and I am the prosecutor for the borough of Brooklyn for the State of New York. I represent the people, and the people are looking for justice for the murder of Mr. Ricardo Desire, a wonderful man who was murdered ten years ago. He was a smart and wealthy man who loved living life to the fullest and who absolutely adored his kids. The only problem he had was loving two women at the same time. We know that was really messed up; however, we must not judge his heart. We all have somehow caused another person some kind of heartache, but does that mean we must be killed for that? This case is definitely not going to be judged on Mr. Ricardo Desire's actions but on his cold-hearted murderer's actions who killed him ten years ago and tried to make it look like a suicide. Yes. The defendant is a decorated detective, but don't let that confuse you from seeing the facts. Let's do right by Mr. Ricardo Desire."

He walked away, and then Kim stood up.

"Good morning, ladies and gentlemen of the jury. My name is Attorney Kimberly Jacobson, and I represent the defendant, the highly decorated Connecticut Detective Andre Brown. You will hear about a young man who felt he and his family, especially his mother, were being used by Mr. Ricardo Desire during his twisted love triangle. Detective Andre Brown just wanted to talk with Mr. Ricardo Desire, but Mr. Ricardo Desire had other plans. You'll see the truth. Thank you."

Kim sat down, and I knew Andre finally talked with Kim, but when? I told her to let me know when he spoke, but I guess it was better for me not to know. Or maybe she was playing dumb with me all along.

Then the judge said, "ADA Becks. Please call your first witness."

"The people call Detective Adam Singleton."

Detective Singleton was sworn in.

"Good morning. Can you state your name for the court, detective?"

"My name is Homicide Detective Adam Singleton."

"Detective Singleton. You were the leading detective on Mr. Ricardo Desire's murder, correct?"

"I was."

"Please tell us what you saw, your investigation, and your findings."

"Around one o'clock on the day of the murder, my partner and I received a call from our captain stating to report to a homicide scene in Brooklyn Heights. When we got there, the victim's door was open, and there was a man named Michael Drew standing right inside talking to officers regarding what he saw."

"And what did he see?"

"He stated he saw the door cracked open, and he walked inside and saw the victim lying on his back on the floor with a gun in his left hand pointing at his left temple."

"Did you ask Mr. Michael Drew why he was there?"

"I did. He said he was coming to visit the victim, who was a father figure to him and his friends. But later we found out that he lied about coming by himself. He was there with his friend Mr. Daniel Scott, who fled the scene. Weeks later I talked with him, and he said he left because he doesn't like cops. Both men were ruled out as suspects because their fingerprints weren't found in the home. However, Mr. Daniel Scott's fingerprints were found on the doorknob."

"I have no more questions, Your Honor."

The judge spoke. "Go ahead, Ms. Jacobson."

Kim walked up to the stand. "Good morning, detective. Were any of the fingerprints in the home connected to my client?"

"Not that we know of. But that doesn't mean there weren't any."

"Did you encounter any witnesses who actually placed my client at the scene?"

"No. Not until—"

Kim swiftly cut him off. "Thank you, Detective Singleton. I have no more questions."

The judge said, "Detective Singleton. You may step down. ADA Becks. Call your next witness."

"The people call the Brooklyn Medical Examiner Dr. Steven Wells."

Dr. Wells went to the witness stand, was sworn in, and sat down.

"Good morning, Dr. Wells. From your findings, how did the victim die?"

"Although it looked to be a suicide because of the gunshot to the left side of his head, the cause of death was a deep knife wound to the left side into his back. He was bleeding extremely fast."

"What about the bullet from the gun?"

"That came after he died. The victim could not have shot himself because first his hand and gun were exactly by his head. The kickback of that kind of gun is too strong and would have placed his hand in a different position away from his body. It wouldn't be perfectly near his head. Second, his body was perfectly laid on the floor. If he shot himself, his body would have been on his side. It looks like he was laid in that position with assistance. Finally, his hand barely had any gunpowder on it, and that told me that the victim wasn't the shooter."

"Thank you, doctor. I have no more questions."

Kim stood up. "The defense has no questions for the doctor."

Then the judge said, "Thank you, doctor. You may step down. That will be it for today, ladies and gentlemen of the jury. Court is adjourned."

We got up, and Jane and I blew kisses at Andre and waved

goodbye to him. We walked out of the courtroom, and the press were in my face, and Kim quickly jumped in. "Today was a good and informative day. Tomorrow will be even better."

We walked away, and I thanked Kim, and we all jumped into her car back to Connecticut. The next morning Kim picked us up, and we went and sat in the courtroom. The judge entered the courtroom with morning greetings, and he told ADA Becks to call his first witness.

"The people call Ms. Renee Parker to the stand."

She was sworn in.

"Ms. Parker. Can you tell the court who Mr. Ricardo Desire was?"

"Ric was a fun-loving and great-looking man. Everyone loved him. He was quiet and well mannered. His only flaw that I knew of was him loving two women."

"Sounds like the world missed him the last ten years?"

"Definitely. But we missed him before that once he separated from my sister."

ADA Becks quickly interrupted her. "I have no further questions."

That threw ADA Becks for a loop because she showed the court he was out of the picture before, and we wanted to know why. Kim pounced on that moment. Kim walked toward the jury, looked at them, and asked her,

"How many years before his death was Mr. Ricardo Desire missing? You know, out of the picture?"

"Oh, I definitely would say more than five. I didn't know their relationship, but I think they loved each other."

"Oh, really? People who know me know I love my daughters and know I love my dogs. They don't think that I do. Tell us, how many times have you heard your sister say she hated Mr.

Ricardo Desire or she wanted to kill him?"

ADA Becks knew Kim tricked Renee.

"Many times. She committed suicide because of him. You know what, I—"

Kim cut her off.

"I have no other questions for Ms. Parker, Your Honor."

The judge looked at Renee and stated she could step down. Then he told Kim to call her witness.

"The defense calls Captain Mike Peters to the stand."

After being sworn in, he sat down.

"Good morning, Captain Peters. Please tell us how you know the defendant."

"I have known Detective Andre Brown for eight years when he started working at my police station. He has been the best detective I ever had the privilege to have in my squad."

"What made him the best?"

"Well, we never received a complaint about him from either the criminals he arrested or from his colleagues. Detective Brown only received compliments. Not only is he highly decorated, he stood out at a time when there were a few corrupt officers and detectives in my squad. Detective Brown is nothing less than the best crime fighter I ever witnessed."

"I have no more questions, Your Honor."

ADA Becks stood up and walked over to Captain Peters.

"One question. You mean to tell the people and the jury that at no time during the corruption in your squad Detective Brown never knew or was involved in anything corrupt?"

"Look. He wasn't a dirty detective. I did bad things and was associated with criminals who can touch almost anyone, even people like you, ADA Becks. But Detective Brown is squared away. Now, are we done here, ADA Becks?"

ADA Becks walked away. "I have no further questions."

Kim stood up, "Your Honor, the defense calls Mrs. Laura Brown to the stand."

I nervously stood up, walked over, and was sworn in.

"Mrs. Brown. Tell us how you met your husband, Detective Andre Brown."

"We met on a plane heading to Georgia. Ironically, I was on standby, and the passenger never showed up, so I was given the seat, and it happened to be next to Andre. We started talking, and we discovered we were headed to the same place. He was an undergrad, and I was a graduate student both at Georgia Southern University. I loved him from the moment I saw and talked with him."

"Please tell the court about your life with him."

"I honestly really love my husband. He is the father of our beautiful daughters. He is a provider, a lover, a shoulder to lean and cry on, and my rock. For ten years, he has given me nothing short of happiness and surprises. I have a man who loves telling the world he's comfortable with loving one woman. He has always been wonderful. I think the criminals he arrested would say he wasn't a bad or crooked detective."

"Did you know about the crime he's accused of?"

"I had no clue until Detectives Jackson and Whitehead arrested him. He never, and I mean he never, talked about his parents. He never talked about having siblings or anything like that."

"The defense rests, Your Honor."

ADA Becks stood up. "The people have no questions at this time for this witness, Your Honor."

As he sat down and the judge said I was excused, I felt happy but disappointed. I helped Andre, but did I really want to? I was confused.

Chapter Twelve

The next morning we arrived at court, and after we waited for the judge to come in, we sat, and he told ADA Becks to call his witness.

"The state calls Mr. Daniel Scott to the stand."

Daniel walked up, placed his hand on the Bible, and was sworn in. He looked relatively healthy. He looked clean and was eating well in witness protection, which I still didn't understand why he was in there. I sat back and watched Daniel's testimony.

"Good morning, Mr. Scott. Tell us how you know the defendant."

"I have known Detective Andre Brown since the day he was born. Actually, his real name is Greg Smith, named after his father."

The entire courtroom looked on with shock. Why didn't I know that?

ADA Becks said,

"Real name? What do you mean?"

"You know. He must have changed his name after he left Brooklyn."

"Would you know why Detective Andre Brown would change his name?"

"I guess to hide who he was just in case the cops were looking for him."

"Why would the cops come looking for him? Tell us the history you have with him and how and why you are here today."

"I grew up with his older brother, James, since we were around five years old. Andre is three years younger. James and I also grew up with another friend our age. We were tight as hell, but we all had family issues. It was James, me, and Michael Drew, and when we turned seven, Diane Downs became tight with us. Diane's father was chasing his wife around in the streets to help change her life around from smoking crack. My pops and Michael's pops were laid off from the meat-manufacturing company, and my pops went on to become a drug dealer. Michael's parents started using crack, and soon even James's pops started smoking crack with Michael's parents. Before being laid off, all three of them were married and had a tight-nested group of friends. But of course, when crack hit, it destroyed those couples.

One night James was home cooking for him and his little brother. His mother came home from work just to see her piece of shit boyfriend on the couch doing nothing. They argued and started fighting, and James picked up a boiling pot of water and threw it on the dude, who received third-degree burns. In the process, his mother and little brother also got hot water on them. His mother was burned on her hand and his little brother was burned on the back of his leg near his ankle, probably eight inches long.

Time went by, and we all turned twenty-seven during the same month. We went to James's grandmother's house to see him and tried to celebrate our birthdays together. He wasn't there, but his aunt Carol and grandmother were. They told us that he was doing really bad. At the time, Michael was about to get married, and I was smoking crack. She asked us if we could talk to him to turn his life around. We agreed and left. I told Michael that we needed to find where Mr. Ricardo lived at to get James back on his feet. We loved Mr. Ricardo because he was a treasure. A week later, Michael told me that he heard that Mr. Ricardo came back from the DR and he had his address.

The next day we met up at James's grandmother's house and James wasn't there. We sat on the couch, and Michael told James's aunt and grandmother our plans and the address where Mr. Ricardo lived. At that same time, the defendant Greg, I mean Andre, entered the living room from one of the rooms in the back and stood there while we talked. Then he left the room and went into the bathroom. The next morning Michael and I went back to James's grandmother's house and the cops were there. We turned around and went to see Mr. Ricardo at his brownstone. We couldn't find parking, so we parked a block away. We started walking towards Mr. Ricardo's home, and when we got to the corner, we saw a young Black male coming out the front door and walking fast going toward the next corner. He had on a black hoodie, black sneakers, and black shorts but no socks. I saw his ankle, and it was scarred. It was James's little brother, Greg. I didn't say anything to Michael about it. I don't even think he noticed Greg. We walked up to Mr. Ricardo's house, and the door wasn't fully closed. I yelled out to Mr. Ricardo who we were, but we didn't receive any response.

We went in and quickly saw him on the floor dead with a gun in his hand. Michael called the police, and I left and sat in Michael's car before they arrived. It was the ugliest scene I ever saw. He was lying in his pool of blood and with a gunshot to the head. I couldn't tell the police who I think did it, but come on, man! He was one of the few who knew the address and has a scar on his ankle. I never would have thought in a million years Mr. Ricardo would've committed suicide or even the defendant would have ever did this crime. I couldn't believe it. Greg, I mean Andre, was a smart dude. He finished high school, went to college, and made something of himself. He wasn't a street kind of guy."

ADA Becks walked away and slowly shook his head, displaying his disgust that Daniel just said too much.

"Thank you. No further questions."

"Your witness, Ms. Jacobson."

"Thank you, Your Honor. Mr. Scott, please tell us what happened to you."

Before he started to answer, I heard someone getting up, and I turned around, and I saw Detective Jackson walking out.

Daniel started talking, "I had a rough road. I started in the streets smoking weed, and I graduated to crack. I committed many crimes, and I'm not proud of it, and I own it. I have never been in trouble with the law, and I don't lie."

"Ok, Mr. Scott. Did you see my client's face at the crime scene?"

"No. I did not."

"Did you address the crime scene with anyone?"

"No. I did not."

"Did you even secretly call the police and leave a tip of the crime? As a matter of fact, you left the scene refusing to talk to the police, leaving your friend Mr. Michael Drew to tell the story himself. Forcing him to lie to the cops about why he was there and whether he was by himself. We talked to Mr. Michael Drew, and do you know what he told us? He said you were a coward then and a coward now. That you were and will always be a crack addict. He told us that you are a liar, a cheat, and a thief. He told me to ask you to give me the fifty dollars you stole out of his car that day you were at the crime scene. Really? You stole money from your childhood friend for what? What did you use it for? Why did you run? Because he would've found out you were a thief and a liar?"

"No. I ran because I looked like a crack addict. I had crack and my favorite crack pipe in my pocket. I didn't want them to somehow check me. And I never forgot that money and the other people's money I stole. But a liar I'm not. The hell with you."

"Clearly if your closest childhood friend doesn't believe you or trust you, the jury definitely can't. By the way, why are you in witness protection? Wait, don't answer that. You probably lied to get in there for the free meals. I'm done with this witness, Your Honor."

She walked away and looked at me and Jane with the "we are winning this case" look.

Chapter Thirteen

The next day we went to court, and it was Andre's day to take the stand. As we were standing waiting for the judge to enter the courtroom and tell us to be seated, I stood there thinking how this chapter of our lives would end. The judge arrived and told us to be seated. I knew the jury would see Andre as the great-looking man he was, and they would take that into consideration. A man without even a blemish on his career. But deep down inside, I wanted them to believe he was somehow secretly a scumbag. I was conflicted. The judge asked Kim if she was ready to have my husband take the stand.

"Good morning, Your Honor. The defense calls Detective Andre Brown to the stand."

Andre stood up, turned around, smiled at me and Jane, and looked cool and calm as only he could be. He has been in the hot seat many times before testifying as a lead detective, and most importantly, he has been practicing for this moment since the day he killed my father.

"First things first. Let's tackle the elephant in the courtroom. Detective Brown, why did you change your name?"

Andre said with a smooth and calm tone,

"I changed my name to Andre Brown not because I was

running away from my father's history or even ashamed of my name but because I knew that name was too common to narrow down if the police were looking to arrest me."

Everyone in the courtroom couldn't believe it. At that moment, he gave himself up. I won and lost at the same time. He was done!

"I always knew I wanted to become a detective, so I thought Andre Brown would not be in the database as a person of interest."

Kim looked puzzled.

"You admit to killing Mr. Ricardo Desire?"

"Yes."

"I don't believe you. The people of the great State of New York, and each person on this jury, don't believe you. We think you are taking the fall for someone else. We heard testimony even from the person who testified against you that you were a nerd and not even a hateful criminal bone in your body. You're a crime fighter. He stated he never would've believed you would ever hurt Mr. Ricardo Desire. Your wife and your captain raved about you being the best man and detective they ever knew. The state and I talked to the criminals you arrested, and not one complaint. I actually thought they wanted me to get your autograph for them. We heard testimony that Mr. Ricardo Desire was loved and hated. His own sister-in-law stated his wife said several times she wanted to kill him. We could just imagine the number of men who probably were jealous of him. And you want us to believe you actually killed Mr. Ricardo Desire. We're not buying that story. No further questions, Your Honor."

ADA Becks stood up.

"So, since you did it, tell us how Detective Brown. Why are we here? Tell us everything, we're all listening. But first, why did you go see the victim, Mr. Ricardo Desire?"

Before Andre said a word, ADA Becks continued,

"Let me tell you what I think. I think after your grandmother informed you that you were the victim's son, you wanted revenge, and you visited him with the intention to kill him. Or maybe it was your mother who broke the news to you being a bastard son? Isn't it true that you became so enraged when you confronted Mr. Ricardo Desire about being his bastard son that you killed him?"

ADA Becks was trying to show that Andre had some kind of intent of killing my father.

Andre said with a low voice, "No."

"Really? Isn't it true you didn't like what the truth was, so you stabbed Mr. Ricardo Desire and made it look like a suicide?"

Andre said in a low voice, "It wasn't like that."

Andre's short answers were eating ADA Becks alive, and ADA Becks became angry.

"Sir, you had to know that Mr. Ricardo Desire was your biological father. He had to tell you that. He went to the Dominican Republic and officially put you, his daughter, and his other son in his will and with protective rights. We found the signed official paperwork in Mr. Ricardo Desire's home."

I sat there stunned. Did Andre know that Ricardo was my father? Did I marry my brother?

ADA Becks continued, "In the two countries where his family has wealth and a strong political presence, are you not protected by the Dominican and Haitian authorities?"

Andre again said in a low voice, "No."

"You mean to tell me that you only went over there to talk with Mr. Ricardo Desire because of some bogus reason, and you weren't mad once you found out you could've lived a much better life if you were treated like his real son?"

Andre snapped and screamed, "Yes! Fuck them all. You don't know what you're talking about. I hated that I was laughed at because of my father Greg's actions. I hated the fact that he was a crack addict. I was ashamed of him."

Andre turned and talked to the jury.

"I'll tell you the truth. I found out from Michael and Daniel where Ricardo lived the day they came to my grandmother's house while I was on break from college. I wanted to talk to him and ask him why he left my mother and tell him the damage he did to her and to us. I had no intention of hurting or even killing him. He let me in, and we hugged each other. He still wasn't unpacked yet because there were boxes everywhere. He asked if I wanted something to drink, and I said a glass of water would be great, then we sat next to each other. He said in his calm and cool, laid–back ladies' man voice,

'Oh, man, Greg. Look at you, a grown man. I had eyes on you and your brother for many years. Damn! I remember when you were born. I'm so glad you found me. I didn't know anyone knew I came back. Tell me, Greg, how is your mother?'

I said to him in a spiteful tone,

"My mother is not doing well at all. My grandmother had to check her into a mental institution. She has been distraught to say the least ever since you left us. Wait, you said you remember when I was born? How was that? We first met when I was just a kid."

He said, 'I remember you ever since you were in your mother's belly. I recently got an email from Barbara's sister Carol stating she wanted me to meet with her so I could visit Barbara, and she attached a copy of a paternity test.'

He walked over to one of the opened boxes and handed me

two documents.

Then he said, 'I was disappointed that you weren't my son. James is actually my son. It seems that your mother always knew, but Carol didn't. I met your mother in college, we were in love, and she became pregnant. Carol never saw or met me because your mother and I never got the chance to become a known couple. None of our family members met or saw pictures of either one of us until that afternoon when we saw Tracy's sister Renee. I guess your mother took my hair and toothbrushes as DNA samples.'

I was shocked and felt ashamed that I never knew. Ricardo continued in his slow, captivating voice,

'I'm sorry to hear that Barbara is still not doing any better. I will contact Carol and go see her again. Barbara and I loved spending time together. I will visit her sometime this week.'

I looked at him and said, "Ricardo, I have some questions. If you thought I was your son, why did you just come into our lives as young men, leave, and destroy us? How can a man so beautiful inside and outside leave us and stop caring about us?"

I never knew anything about Ricardo's and my mother's past relationship in college. All I knew was that he was greater than my father was, and we really took to him. He was all we wanted in a father. Ricardo looked at the floor and slowly raised his head up with a cowardly expression to look at me and said,

'Greg. I couldn't stay around. I was married to another woman, and I had children. I have a daughter the same age as James, and I have a son your age. Look. Maybe your mother didn't explain the history between her and me to you and James, but you're a man now, and I cannot be looked at as the bad guy. Your mother and I met while we were in college. We were in classes together. We were meant for each other, but the timing wasn't right. Later she married Greg Sr. She wanted to give it a chance, but she loved me and Greg. I followed her everywhere she went, but I never wanted her to know. Your father was a good guy and never cheated on your mother. He was overprotective of her, so much so that he didn't pay attention to her. He barely talked to her, and I became the shoulder she leaned on, continuing our affair. It was a secret and wonderful relationship, but my wife, Tracy, started to be suspicious of me having affairs because women always came around me. She knew about your mother but not the affair. Tracy is one of the greatest women I know. Her personality lights up a room. She didn't go to college, and she isn't the smartest person to be around, but she was very seductive and sexy. Then your mother got pregnant three years later with you. Years later I came and lived with all of you until we ran into Renee. Your mother, Tracy, and I needed a break. We all were entangled in a twisted love triangle. Your mother with me and Greg Sr., and me with your mother and Tracy. I moved away from my wife and family, and I went to a place to be by myself, to clear my head. Thinking I was helping people in my life, now I know leaving hurt the ones I loved.'

Then he walked to the kitchen area, standing by the island. I was confused and mad at him and about the history of my parents. Then I got up and walked toward him and asked,

"All those times you were with my mother, why did you let her suffer physically, emotionally, and financially?"

He angrily snapped at me. 'Your mother refused my help, but the times I was there, I made sure you and James received everything you both wanted.'

I angrily snapped back at him. "Do you know James loves you to death?"

He shook his head, 'I know. I love him even when I thought he wasn't my son. But watching both of you grow up, I truly believe he couldn't be my son.'

At that moment, I really was getting very upset at Ricardo, and I should've left, but I decided to see what he was talking about. So I asked him,

"What do you mean by that?"

He stared at me and said, 'Me, you, and my other children are quiet, smart, and intelligent people. We crave understanding and education. We have a glow about us. We are strong and resilient, but James is not. James lacks that glow, or any glow for that matter. He doesn't think about his actions. He lacks the confidence and the intelligence that my kids have.'

This bastard! He was insulting my brother. My brother who taught me everything and served as my father for almost my entire life. My brother who fed me and our mother when Ricardo just watched from a distance. Ricardo was angering me by discrediting James. Then he turned his head around and gave me this "Come on, you know James is dumb" look, and it was too much for me to take. Before he fully turned around, he said,

'One of the reasons I was in the Dominican Republic was to make sure all my kids had—'

I picked up one of the knives that was on the island, and I stabbed that piece of shit right in his left side and swiftly turned it maybe three times. He yelled and yelled for help, sort of what my mother did when he left her. I violently pulled the knife out, placed it in my pocket, and threw him on the ground on his back. While he was bleeding fast, I went into his bedroom, slammed the door, and was looking through his things. In the second opened box, I found a gun. I never touched or used a gun before, so I took it, left the room, I placed the gun in his left hand, put it by his head, and at that moment, he turned his head, he looked at me, and instead of me stopping and crying, I shot him. I rushed out the front door, swiftly walked to the nearest bus stop, jumped on the bus, and went to my grandmother's house. I couldn't believe I killed the man I loved."

I cried as I was holding Jane and looking at Andre wiping his tears from his face. The courtroom was completely silent, so much so that you could hear the tears drop from the faces of the jury. The bastard really killed my father. Then ADA Becks broke the silence by clapping.

"What a great performance, my heart bleeds for you. Is there anything else you wish to add to your confession? Especially since you are going to die in prison."

I couldn't believe Kim was letting Andre continue to hang himself.

Andre looked at ADA Becks.

"Then a week later I went to Ricardo's funeral with my mother and James, but before we all went inside to see Ricardo in the casket, I started crying because I killed the man I loved, which also was one of the men I hated. I went into the bathroom for a few minutes to collect myself, then I left the bathroom and went straight outside, and a few minutes later James and my mother came out and said to me that we had to go. For weeks, I lived on the edge, staying in my room at my grandmother's home acting like I was studying for the upcoming semester. Then the day came, and I got on a plane at JFK and happened to sit next to my future wife."

An irate ADA Becks asked,

"Why didn't you tell your loving wife at least about any of your family history?"

"I couldn't tell anyone. I was scared. I didn't know if anyone would connect the dots and turn me in. I would have been arrested, and it would have caused my mother tremendous pain knowing I killed the love of her life. I changed my major from business to criminal justice. I wanted to be the one who solved crimes and murders, bringing closure to families, and I did that."

"I don't believe you. I think your primary goal for seeing the victim was to intentionally kill him for the pain he caused already. And once you found out that the victim already made you a beneficiary and officially his son with the Haitian and Dominican Republic political parties, you killed him. It wasn't over this heat-of-the-moment crap you're trying to feed us."

"You don't know what you're talking about. I'm not his son!"

"When the cops arrested you, you had in your wallet a New York state driver's license with Greg Smith's name on it. Why did you keep that? Why not shred it? I know. You were keeping it to later prove your claim of inheritance, then switch back to Detective Andre Brown."

"Look! I don't know anything about that. I just forgot it was in my wallet."

"Really? How was that when it was right behind your Connecticut driver's license? You never had to take your license out to show someone?"

"No. I did not."

"I can understand you forgot about it when you got your Georgia driver's license, but I can't understand how you did not see it when you turned in your Georgia driver's license when you first received your Connecticut driver's license."

ADA Becks demonstrated with his own wallet, showing to the jury that Andre and any other person on this earth would not have missed it. ADA Becks continued,

"You know what, don't answer that. We all are tired of your pile of excuses. Tell us, detective, why would your friend Mr. Daniel Scott be scared and ask for witness protection?"

"I don't know. Maybe because I'm a cop. Maybe he's a liar, or maybe you told him about Ricardo's family and he became scared. There is no telling what you have told him. But like I said, I'm not his son."

An angry but very satisfied ADA Becks said to the judge,

"I'm done with Detective Brown, Your Honor."

"That's it for today. We will convene tomorrow."

We blew kisses to Andre and told him to hold on. Kim, Jane, and I walked out of the courtroom, and Kim said to me,

"Laura. Did you know any of this?"

"Hell no! This is crazy."

"We got killed in there today."

"I know you have a game plan, but it sure didn't look like it was working."

"Yes. What a long day."

Jane and I left Kim and got lunch before heading back to Connecticut.

The next morning after we sat down, ADA Becks asked the court if the people could recall a witness. The judge nodded, and then ADA Becks said,

"The people call Laura Brown to the stand."

What the hell was this? I wasn't ready and was extremely indecisive. Will I be the one to save him or be the one who sinks him? Once again, the judge gave the order to mute or turn off phones in the courtroom. Before ADA Becks stood up to walk to me, he turned around, and Detective Jackson walked into the courtroom, and he turned toward her. She handed him a paper, and he looked at it.

"Your Honor, may I approach?"

The judge nodded. ADA Becks and Kim walked up to the judge, and ADA Becks said,

"Your Honor. The people just received new evidence that we need to prepare for. Obviously, we will share this with the defense."

"That's fine. Make a copy for Ms. Jacobson, and the both of you have until one o'clock to be ready." Then he addressed the court.

"Everyone. We will convene at one o'clock. Mrs. Brown, you may step down and come back to take the stand when we come back. Court is in recess."

I got up and walked to Kim.

"What the fuck is going on?"

"I don't know, but when I do, I'll call you. Let me find out what's going on. Take Jane for something to eat."

Jane and I left, found a restaurant, and waited around twenty minutes for a table. We sat down, looked at menus, and ordered.

"Mommy. I'm so tired of this. Why are people trying to destroy our family and take my father away? This world is so terrible."

"Jane. You will learn that one minute you are on top of the world, and the next minute you are forced into the flames. You'll always have to be ready to help your sisters because whether your father comes out of this innocent or not, we will all need your strength."

Our food arrived, and we started eating and continued talking.

"I know, Mommy, and I'm holding strong for us, but one day can you and Daddy tell me about the past and our family history?"

While she was talking, my phone was buzzing, and I knew it

was Kim calling me. However, knowing what Jane was going through, I couldn't interrupt her at that moment. I told myself, I will look at my phone as soon as we finish eating and leave. Once we were finished, I looked at my watch, and it was twelve thirty.

"Wow! Look at the time. We have to get back. Waitress, check, please."

After waiting for our check while our waitress tried to sell more food to us, I paid the bill, and we left. With us walking fast, going through security, and rushing back into the courtroom, I didn't have any time to talk with Kim or look at my phone. It was exactly one o'clock, and I walked past Kim and straight to the stand. I was sworn back in, and before I sat down, I looked at Kim, and she shook her head, whispering,

"I'm sorry."

Oh shit! What's happening?

"Your Honor. May I please have a moment with my attorney?"

"No, Mrs. Brown. First of all, she is not your attorney, and second, you had enough time to consult with the defense attorney for your husband. ADA Becks, please proceed."

"Thank you, Your Honor. Mrs. Brown. You said that you knew nothing of your husband's past, correct?"

"Correct."

"So, did you ever ask him about any past events or greatest moments of his life before marrying you?"

"No. I never wanted to push him into talking about something that he might have horrible memories about."

"So, you never asked about old flames or just grandmothers, health issues, or anything of that nature?"

"That's right."

"Ok. You said both of you met by luck, correct? On the same

plane with you as a standby. Just got lucky, correct?"

"Correct."

I saw Kim trying her best not to be seen giving me hints of what I was being set up for.

"Ok. Do you know a person named Douglass? If you do, who is he?"

I couldn't lie about knowing Douglass because he was my cousin, and now I was being overwhelmed and overpowered. Everything that I did to prepare for this moment was going down the drain. My head was starting to spin very fast, and I was thinking about fainting to get a break, but the question took over the moment. I knew this was turning into Double D's story. But they had nothing.

"He was my cousin who died years ago. Why are you asking me about him?"

"I'll ask the questions here, Mrs. Brown. Do you know a man named Justice? And who is he?"

"He was Douglass's friend. He introduced us when I stayed in New York during my father's funeral."

"According to their rap sheets, these two were hard criminals with robbery and attempted murder cases. Why would a highly educated person like yourself associate with those guys? You didn't live in their world."

"I don't know. It just happened."

"So, again, you were at the right place at the right time. Ok. We'll get back to that. Now, what is your connection to Diane Downs?"

"Who?"

"I'm sorry. You may know her by her street name, Double D? Remember, Mr. Scott testified that he grew up with Ms. Downs."

"Listen. I don't know Mr. Scott or Ms. Downs."

"Really? Then why did you pay a private investigator to find her? You know Ms. Sarah Mitchell. The one who accepts only cash to avoid paying her deadbeat husband alimony."

I was stuck for words. How did they get to Sarah? I bet because she was walking around in the hood asking around, and Detectives Jackson and Whitehead asked the same people and gave them cash or a get-out-of-jail-free card. Was all of this on the paper Detective Jackson gave to ADA Becks earlier this morning?

"Ok. You're not in the right place this time, right? Fine, if you don't know Ms. Downs but you paid to have her found, and obviously you became disappointed to know she killed herself, so how can you explain the letter she wrote claiming you paid to have Douglass, Justice, and her set up and kill your wonderful husband's beloved brother, James Smith, for five dollars? Your Honor, I submit exhibit A to you and to the court."

As I sat there shocked, the bastard handed copies to the members of the jury. I looked at Andre, and he was crying, then he yelled,

"Why?"

As the judge, jury, and Andre read the letter, I sat trembling in silence. My truth was set free, and I hurt the man I loved. I had my own half brother killed, and you know what, I would do it again. I didn't know that five dollars was a payment! But I couldn't say that because I broke my husband's heart.

"I have no further questions."

Kim stood up.

"Your Honor. Can I redirect?"

He nodded.

"You paid violent street thugs to murder your husband's only brother, who's also your half brother?"

Andre jumped up and yelled,

"YOUR FUCKING FATHER!"

The judge told him to sit down.

Kim continued,

"Then on the day you had him killed, you just happened to get a seat on a plane as a standby next to the man who loved and took care of you for ten years? What was your endgame?"

I was shocked that she was coming at me so hard. I couldn't believe it. Was she mad at me because I hired another private investigator? While I was dazed by her verbal punches hitting my head, she kept going for the kill.

ADA Becks stated "Your Honor. She is badgering the witness."

"It's her own witness."

Then she said to me,

"So, while you were in New York paying and plotting to kill James Smith for five dollars, how can you convince us that you didn't kill your father for the insurance and the inheritance money? You could have definitely been in New York before he died. You are the oldest, and you claimed you loved him. We can understand why Andre never talked about his past, but what is your excuse? Were you scared that he would have left you or maybe turned you in?"

I finally broke down, thinking that was what she wanted me to do. I cried and screamed,

"I was running from my past and family! I didn't want anyone to know about my faults."

"Seems to me that your marriage was built on lies you created. I believe you told him you killed your father and now you have this highly decorated detective lying to protect the woman he loves. It wouldn't be the first time a spouse has done that. The defense rests, Your Honor."

"You are excused, Mrs. Brown."

I got up, quickly walked past Kim and Andre, reached out for Jane's hand, and grabbed it, and we rushed out of the courtroom. I flagged down a cab, and we took it to the train station and went home. While we were on the train, I looked at my phone and saw I missed seven calls and a text message stating,

WE HAVE TO MEET NOW!!!!

I looked at Jane, and instead of yelling at her about my reason for not picking up my phone while we were eating, I thought about the verbal abuse my mother did to me, and I never wanted any of my girls to feel like I did, and I didn't want to become like my mother. I pulled her toward me, hugged her, and cried. Later that night Kim called me.

"Laura. I want you to know the reason I went at you today. I did it to let the jury know that there was a possibility that even though he confessed to the crime, Andre did not kill Ricardo. That someone else did. That puts reasonable doubt in some of the jury members' minds. Although it was a rough moment, I believe we helped his cause. Laura, I believe your marriage is over. It is because there isn't any trust between the two of you anymore. As I said in court, your marriage was built on lies, and they rose to the surface once he was arrested."

"I know, Kim."

"The morning after you informed me that you couldn't afford my investigator anymore, Andre called me and asked how the case was going. I told him that I had nothing, and that you told me to stop using my investigator because you couldn't afford it. He told me that a few of his fellow detectives created a fund for him, and instead of giving it to you, that I could have it for my investigator. He also asked me not to tell you about it because you were already stressed out.

I received the money and gave it to my investigator, and she searched into Ricardo's life, reaching out to his mother in the Dominican Republic. Of course, others reached out to her before, and she refused to talk with them because she believed the US government didn't care to solve her son's murder, but my investigator had the golden key, as she spoke Spanish, and his mother felt comfortable with that. She flew down to the Dominican Republic and met with Ricardo's mother. My investigator arrived back in the States, and while she was telling me what she learned, she asked me for my assistance with the best way of locating a woman for one of her clients. After I told her what she could do, she accidentally stated her client's name was Laura Brown, and my investigator's name is Sarah Mitchell—you know, the one you hired behind my back. She did a good job, but her mistake was giving out her business cards to people hoping to get information. One of them was an informant, and that's how the detectives traced everything back to you. I knew about the note Diane's boyfriend gave Sarah but not the entire letter he provided the detectives with. And since Andre wasn't talking and you told me not to involve you, I kept the note to myself until this morning when Detective Jackson handed the entire letter to ADA Becks. By the time he showed it to me, I knew I had to warn you, but you didn't answer my calls or my text message. Look, I know this day has been painful and stressful, but do you have any questions for me?"

"No. Thank you for everything. I will see you tomorrow morning."

I hung up and couldn't go to sleep. I hurt my husband so badly, but I needed and wanted him home. It was my job to take care of him. The next morning, I left Jane and the girls with a neighbor whose daughters are friends with the girls. I didn't want to bring Jane anymore because I felt she had enough. I drove my car and went to court for closing arguments, and Kim went first.

She stood up and walked over to the jury.

"Good morning, ladies and gentlemen of the jury. I know this case has taken a toll on you. At times straightforward and other times confusing. But make no mistake about it, the only thing that is straight in this case is that the people haven't proved without a shadow of a doubt that Detective Andre Brown did murder Mr. Ricardo Desire. Of course, he confessed, but the loving and kindhearted man he is, I truly feel he is taking the rap for someone else and you do too. He has been lied to from the day he was born, even during his perfect ten-year marriage. But let's forget that for a minute. The people's primary witness is a thief and liar, and we showed that his wife, Laura, could have killed her father. This is plain and simple. If you can't one hundred percent believe Detective Andre Brown is the killer, then you cannot convict him. Thank you, ladies and gentlemen of the jury."

Then ADA Becks stood up, and he walked over to the jury.

"In life, we all will have a moment where we will need to make a crucial decision, and on that summer day in Brooklyn, Detective Andre Brown made a terrible decision. From his own mouth, he purposely went to the victim's house and murdered him after learning that was his brother's father. He could have easily left, informed his brother, and their lives could have changed. Who knows, maybe both Mr. Ricardo Desire and his son Mr. James Smith would be alive today. Then he staged the scene so someone else could be blamed and sit in prison for life. This is not the loving, wonderful, and kindhearted man we all heard about! Then he fled the scene and even went to Mr. Ricardo Desire's funeral. Ignore all the noise, distractions, and great praise for Detective Andre Brown. He is the murderer who legally changed his name and kept an old driver's license in case he needed to cash in on his beneficiary money or leave the country. Let's provide him a passport to Attica for twenty-five years to life, showing him and other criminals justice doesn't hide behind a handsome man with a badge. Don't send Detective Andre Brown back home to Connecticut—send him to prison. Thank you, ladies and gentlemen of the jury."

He walked back to his chair, and the judge dismissed the jury and the court until a verdict was made. I waited in Brooklyn for hours until Kim called me and told me the verdict was in. Everyone returned to the courtroom and stood until the bailiff introduced the judge, who instructed everyone to sit.

"Good afternoon, ladies and gentlemen of the jury. Foreman, do you have a verdict?"

"We do, Your Honor."

"What say you?"

"We the jury in the case of the people of the State of New York versus Andre Brown in the charge of murder in the first degree say not guilty."

The courtroom was in awe, and we hugged Andre and thanked Kim. The judge thanked the jury for their service, and everyone started leaving the courtroom. After talking to the press, Andre looked at me, and we smiled at each other. We jumped into our car, went to eat, talked about celebrating that night, and headed home. Before we left New York, I asked my neighbor if the girls could spend the night because Andre and I wanted to spend his first night home together alone, and she texted me back that would be great.

"Andre baby. Irma, our neighbor, will have the girls stay over at her house tonight."

"That's great, baby. We can play catch up and get back where we left off."

We were excited! Next thing I knew we arrived in front of our home. We kissed, and we continued until we got inside.

IV

Part Four

Olena

What I have learned is there is drama that comes with loving that man. Lives collide and lives are destroyed. I call it Ricardo's Collisions, and there are consequences with being connected to him.

<u>Character List</u>

Olena: Detective/main character/narrator
Barbara: Olena's aunt/James's mother
Tiffany: Olena's twin sister/paramedic
James: Olena's cousin
Carol: Olena's mother
Ricardo: Laura's father
Renee: Tracy's sister
Alex: Laura's brother
Douglass: Laura's cousin
Daniel: James's friend

Chapter Fourteen

All units to respond. Reported shooting of a Black male in his twenties on East Fifty-Second and Snyder Avenue.

"Dispatch. We got it."

As I sat in the passenger seat while my partner drove to our first shooting of the day, racing and speeding in and out of traffic with the siren pounding the ears of everyone nearby, I thought to myself why I never knew my father. It's times like these that make me think that I wouldn't be in this profession if I knew my father or even had one. I'm twenty-four years old, and I never understood the circumstances around my parents' decision, and knowing my mother, they both probably couldn't stand each other.

My great-grandparents met in Costa Rica, and they both came from poor backgrounds. They made the long journey to America, and they settled in Brooklyn and had two daughters. My grandmother is a caring and respectful woman. She took care of people who came to her for help, sometimes for food, sometimes a place to stay, and once in a while for money. People took advantage of her. One time my mother was in a crunch and needed three hundred dollars, but she lied to my grandmother and asked her for a thousand dollars. My mother took an extra seven hundred dollars knowing that she was wrong. Of course, she spent it on clothes and on a man who didn't stay with her. My grandmother is the kind of woman anyone would love to meet.

My aunts Barbara and Janet are great. I never saw any of their shortcomings, but that didn't mean they didn't have them. My aunt Janet is the oldest, and she is nothing short of great. Although she had her share of drama, especially dealing with my mother, she is a goal-oriented and successful oral surgeon. My aunt Barbara is an adjunct law professor and has two sons. She is a highly motivated woman. Both aunts I haven't seen in a while. As a matter of fact, the last I saw my aunt Barbara was when her youngest son was a little boy.

We finally arrived at the scene. I walked up to the paramedics, and one of them was my twin sister, Tiffany, and she was crying.

"What's wrong?"

She grabbed and hugged me as if a nuclear bomb was about to land in our area.

"It's James!"

"James. Our cousin James?"

"Yes. Come and see."

And there he was, my cousin James. He was lying there lifeless as he passed away while Tiffany was trying to save him. We both have been to too many crime scenes, but this was totally different. I became numb. I told her that I will meet her at the hospital, but I had to cover the scene because this was my case. I walked over to the bystanders, asking if anyone saw what happened, and of course, no one ever does. I walked away and went into the supermarket and asked for the manager. He immediately came to me with the security guard and an employee.

"Hello. I'm Detective Olena Jackson. Can you tell me what happened outside your supermarket?"

The manager said, "I cannot, but my security guard and employee can."

The security guard was an older White male in his early sixties.

"I noticed something about him as soon as a woman customer brought him to my attention around ninety minutes ago. She came to me and said that there is a man in the next aisle who looked like he was lost, like he was checked out of life. I told her I would check on it. I walked up to him and asked if he was ok or needed any help, and he said no. So, to make sure he was safe, I watched him periodically, as he was barely putting items in his cart."

I thought to myself that James knew he was going to die. I asked the manager if the supermarket had a camera pointing at the crime scene and if I could see it. He took me to the back of the supermarket inside his small office.

"Please find a seat somewhere. Let me find that moment on the tape, Detective Jackson. There they are."

I looked, and across from the supermarket, there were three men and a woman. Then when James walked across the street, a man walked right behind him, pulled down his mask, covered his face, pointed his gun at James's back, and fired two shots in the left side of his back. The shooter screamed, "Revenge, motherfucker!"

He started to run but stopped and bent over for a few seconds like he had some kind of stomach pain or to catch his breath, then he started running again. He and the four other people across from the supermarket ran in different directions. I thanked the manager and asked him for a copy of the tape. I left his office, walked out of the supermarket, and told the two officers on the scene to start canvassing the area for witnesses. Ten minutes later I left and went to Kings County Hospital to see Tiffany. When I got there, she was distraught and still crying. Although we weren't as close as we used to be when we were children, we saw James periodically. The last time we saw him he supported Tiffany's decision to be a paramedic to save lives, and he called me a crime fighter, and that made me want to fight crime. Now not only do I have to find his killer, but I have to break the news to my aunts and grandmother.

I asked Tiffany what happened when she got the call.

"We got the call, and I grabbed the radio while my partner was driving. At that moment, I felt a strange and crazy feeling in my heart and in the pit of my stomach. This call felt extremely scary. I felt like that only one other time, which was my first-ever call. It was a stabbing between two young men, and one stabbed the other with a screwdriver in the other's neck. Then today we arrived, and there he was. Olena, you have to catch the motherfucker who did this to him."

I left her and went to my grandmother's home and told her and my mother the news, and of course they were in disbelief. I couldn't explain who did it, but I vowed I would find out and bring justice to James's killer. However, I had two things against me. The first was I had no leads, and second, I had to keep my captain in the dark regarding my relationship with James because he would've taken me off the case. I went back to the crime scene, and I could not find anyone willing to talk, and adding to that, I couldn't make out any of the faces on the tape even when I zoomed in. The killer wore all black and a hoodie. I would have to wait until the streets started talking. However, there was a clear view of the man's face James was talking to in the supermarket hours before he was killed, but I didn't know who the man was.

Tiffany and I didn't have a good relationship with our mother, and it was wearing on us. Our mother wanted Tiffany to still change her career, and they argued every time we all got together. She never liked our mother. Honestly, she wasn't a horrible mother, but she was very controlling, especially when it came to my and my sister's lives. We have always been smart. We made straight A's from elementary school through high school. My mother wasn't formally educated or successful as her sisters because of her own issues growing up, and she wanted to make sure that my sister and I wouldn't make the same mistake. During her junior high years, my mother started hanging with the wrong crowd, started cutting classes, and then in high school missed days of school. She loved marching to her own beat, and after going far down the wrong road, she couldn't get back on the right track. She had me and my sister out of wedlock when she was nineteen, and we never knew our father. Honestly, I don't think she even knew who he was. We asked her a few times during our teenage years, but she was always vague. She would say, "Oh. He was a bastard, so it was good you didn't know him anyway," or the famous, "What do you need a father for? I'm all you need!" Tiffany and I stopped asking. However, we all knew the importance of knowing our father—even if he was a scumbag or great dad, we always wanted to know. Although she was rough on us, she did provide, and she found ways to keep us on track. Tiffany and I did graduate college.

After a decade, I finally caught a break in James's cold case. I was sitting at my desk around one o'clock, and I heard a deep and raspy voice say to the desk sergeant, "I'm looking to speak to a homicide detective. I have information on the murder of Mr. Ricardo Desire."

The desk sergeant looked around for a detective, and right behind him was my captain. My captain looked at the man and stated "I'm Captain Speedson. Come this way, sir."

My captain looked at me, "Jackson. Come with me."

I had a strong feeling about this man. The hairs on the back of my neck rose up, and I got chills. The man entered the interrogation room, and my captain, my partner, and I stood outside the two-way glass looking at the man. My captain looked at the both of us,

"Look. This cold case is extremely important. I remember everyone in the higher chain took ass chewings for not even getting leads. I vividly remember watching that moment when I was a young pup. Don't fuck this up."

My partner and I entered the room.

"Good afternoon, sir. I'm Detective Olena Jackson, and this is Detective Donnie Whitehead."

As I walked over to him, he looked like an older thirtysomething, really thin drug user who was in recovery. I just knew this guy knew something.

"Sir, what is your name?"

"Daniel Scott."

"Mr. Scott. Would you like something to drink?"

"Yes. Some water would be good. Thank you."

"We'll get that for you. Now, how can I help you, Mr. Scott?"

"I have something to tell you. I want to get this story off my chest."

I received the cup of water and gave it to him. "Tell us your story."

"I'm coming to you because Mr. Ricardo's case is still unsolved, and I got to get it off my chest. I wasn't a part of it, but I know who murdered him. My friend James Smith's brother Greg killed Mr. Ricardo Desire."

While he was about to continue, my captain entered the room and called us to leave the room. "Let's stop this and put him in protective custody. I will go talk to him."

We watched as our captain sat very close to him and was talking very low. Mr. Scott kept nodding his head, then at the end of the conversation, our captain was loud enough for us to hear.

"Look. These people are well connected and will find and kill you. It would be wise for us to place you in witness protection." Mr. Scott nodded his head, and my captain came out of the room. "Set up the paperwork, and don't talk to him. Make sure nobody talks to him. He can't leave our sight."

We walked him out of the room, he sat at my desk, and my partner walked away and said he had to meet up with someone. I knew Mr. Scott would have something to say about my cousin James Smith if it was the same Greg Smith he talked about.

"Wow! This is a crazy moment, isn't it? But before we move forward, I have to ask you if you know who killed James?"

"My boy James died that same summer. I don't know exactly who killed him, but he had a lot of drama and people who hated him. I was asked by two of my friends, Justice and Douglass, to help find him to settle a score, but I wasn't there when he was killed. They were working with some light-skinned bombshell named Linda, Lauren, Lilly, something like that. My friend Double D called the woman L Boogie."

"What score? And what is Double D's real name?"

"The score was for something James did to L Boogie. And Double D's real name is Diane Downs."

"Diane helped L Boogie settle the score? Where can I find Diane?"

"I don't know her whereabouts because she jumps from place to place. The reasons I never came up here or talked to the police is because I don't trust y'all motherfuckers, and James's little brother is my man, but I can't live with this on my head anymore. That summer was the last I saw him, as I heard he was in college studying law or some criminal shit."

"What is James's brother's full name, again?"

"Greg Smith."

"Do you know their mother's name?"

"Mrs. Barbara, and his aunt's name is Ms. Carol."

Right at that moment I knew I had the right man.

"Thank you for your cooperation, Mr. Scott. Please sign your name right here, and you can be on your merry way to witness protection. We will keep in touch. Also, you do know you will have to testify in court. Will you be able to do that?"

"Sure. No problem."

He walked out of the station with two officers. I knew I would have to start from the beginning, and it would start with my aunt Barbara. I visited my grandmother's house hoping to talk with my aunt Barbara, which I haven't done since I was a teenager. I saw my mother there sitting at the kitchen table, and I sat down across from her.

"Hi, Ma. Can you tell me how I can reach aunt Barbara? I really need to talk with her."

"She's been living in a psychiatric ward for close to a decade. Why do you need to talk to her?"

"I've been placed on the cold case murder of Ricardo Desire, and James's name came up."

She suddenly became excited. "Olena! If you crack this case, your name will carry a lot of weight. He was your aunt Barbara's boyfriend. They broke up, and she went into a really deep depression. She started abusing medication and had a nervous breakdown. We can ask her about that. I only met him once, and until his funeral, I never knew his full name. But I know one thing, he was an extremely fine-ass man who was married and made some good-looking babies. Barbara lucked out with that fine piece of ass. But there is bad that comes with that good."

"What do you mean, Ma?"

"What I have learned is there is drama that comes with loving that man. Lives collide and lives are destroyed. I call it Ricardo's Collisions, and there are consequences with being connected to him. We can go see Barbara in a few minutes. Let me freshen up, and we can go."

I became excited. I knew I was getting closer to solving James's case. Who knew I could have cracked this case years ago just by talking to the woman I really couldn't stand talking to? We arrived to see my aunt Barbara, and to my surprise, she was coherent and excited to see us—well, she was excited to see anyone from the outside world, period. My mother walked over to her.

"Hey, Barbara. I brought your niece to come see you."

"Olena. You're a grown woman now."

"How did you know I wasn't Tiffany?"

"I just took a good guess. How are you? Sit down and talk with me."

I was impressed with her. She was ready to talk and tell me everything. Before I could say another word, she said, "Seems like just yesterday when a young woman came in here trying to pass as my niece, hoping to speak with me."

My mother said to her, "Barb! You never told me this. Was this recently?"

"That woman came right around the time my beautiful

Ricardo was killed. Olena, find the piece of crap who stole the love of my life. Carol, go ask the front desk about that woman before we forget. Olena, girl. You are so pretty. Pass me my brush. I look and feel like a hot mess."

"Aunt Barbara—"

"Baby, please. Call me Aunt Barb."

"Aunt Barb. Can you tell me about your son Greg?"

"Greg, my baby! I haven't seen him since last month. I think he lives in Georgia. I remember when my baby was accepted into GSU. That is Georgia Southern University if you didn't know. I loved when he visited me. He always touches my hand with the burned scar on it and kisses it. I always ask him about the scar on his leg, and he never wants to talk about it. But my oldest, James, hasn't come by in years. I hope he isn't still mad at me. I try not to ask Carol or my mother how my kids are doing because they are my kids and I should know. I didn't even ask Greg about James."

I looked up, and my mother was standing ten feet behind my aunt Barbara, and she shook her head. She kept talking about her life, including her relationships, especially with Ricardo, and as I soaked it all in, I realized something important. This woman has been through so much love and pain. She remembered names and great experiences in her life but did not know that her oldest son was killed. When she finished talking, my mother and I told my aunt Barbara goodbye, and we walked to the front desk and asked to speak to the director. The receptionist called her, and the director came over to us, we introduced ourselves, and she asked us to come with her to her office. We came in and sat down.

"My aunt Barbara said a woman visited her years back, but to our knowledge, only four people are allowed to visit her. Do you happen to still have those logs?"

"I remember that day. I was the receptionist back then. She was a pretty young thing in her mid-twenties. A Black woman. She spoke very well and was very respectful. Unfortunately, we shred all of our paper records every five years."

"Damn!"

"Oh, pretty girl, don't worry. We scanned them into our database in case we had another flood. Let me pull it up."

After a minute, the director smiled and looked at us.

"Please come around and look."

There it was, "L. P.," which backs up the Lauren or Lilly claim. I received a copy of the record, said thank you and our goodbyes, and left. I dropped my mother home, and before I could look up the new information I gathered on Greg, I had to close the two open cases I was currently working on and bring justice and closure to the families.

Chapter Fifteen

After weeks of closing both cases, I forgot about what I learned from my mother and my aunt Barbara. When I remembered, I went into my captain's office.

"Cap. I received a huge tip on the James Smith's cold case. I have to go with it."

He was sitting down, and then he looked up at me.

"I thought I told you to drop everything and only focus on Ricardo Desire's cold case. I need my best detective on this, and you're great at what you do, and most importantly, you're incorruptible."

I nodded and walked away from his office. For years, I have been denied access for clearing James's case, with either no witnesses coming forward or being placed on another case. Other than Daniel Scott's short story that was stopped by my captain, I ran out of hope and started banging my head against multiple dead ends. Then one afternoon on my day off, something in my head told me to check the tristate area criminal and mugshots database for Greg Smith. There were many criminals with that name in New York and in New Jersey, but there were only a few in Connecticut. I shot up there and went to all the metro police stations, and none of the stations had any Greg Smith that felt like my cousin. Then while driving to the last station, I remembered that he went to college for law or criminal justice. I went inside, and there were a few detectives I knew from a joint task force we were on two years ago that involved catching a killer from New York living in Connecticut. I walked up to one of the detectives, we exchanged greetings, and I said, "Hey, how many Greg Smiths do you have in the system?"

"Suspects?"

"Yeah. Let's start there, and we can—"

Then I heard a woman officer say, "Looks like you had a great workout, Detective Andre Brown."

I looked to my right and saw this tall, built Black man wearing a black T-shirt, black shorts, black sneakers, and no socks, and he had a boiling scar on his left ankle. It's him! And he was another detective I knew on that task force. And he is my cousin! But why is his name now Andre Brown? Before I could even talk about him being the killer, I had to know his history, and I didn't want to approach him because he probably would recognize me or become spooked.

I left and drove back to Brooklyn and went to my captain's office.

"Sir. Can we speak privately?"

"Yes. Come on in."

I walked into his office and sat down.

"I have a suspect in the Ricardo Desire's murder. I can do this, but I have to dig into his background. I need a few days to travel, can you approve it?"

"Hell yeah, Jackson. We need this cold case solved."

I got up, went to my desk, and called my mother.

"Ma? What school did Greg go to again?"

"GSU."

"And GSU stands for?"

"Georgia Southern University. He majored in criminal justice."

"Thanks, Ma." I hung up and ran back into my captain's office.

"Sir. I have to go down to Georgia to trace my suspect's steps."

"Close the door and have a seat. Let me tell you something. When this case first happened, I was just an officer trying to survive in these streets. I was truly wet behind the ears. This was a huge case, and big money was thrown at it. The mayor, commissioner, and every captain in the city were looking for the killer. If you truly believe you found your guy, I will get you whatever you need to catch him. You know me. I need this son of a bitch badly. I even give you the credit, but run it by me first, and don't tell anyone but me. Are you driving or need plane tickets?"

"I'm flying."

"Ok. Let's make this happen. Keep me in the loop."

Off I went to GSU. I had to connect the dots between Greg Smith and Andre Brown. I entered the register's office and asked the representative for Andre Brown's records, and there were three of them, and only one of them graduated with a criminal justice degree. I asked to see a picture of him, and again there he was. Then I went to his first police station where he worked as a rookie cop. I asked for the captain there and told him I was looking up information regarding Officer Andre Brown, and for the time Greg was there, nothing but praise and a clean record. I also found out that he moved to Connecticut. I really knew right there the detective I saw that day in Connecticut was my cousin and suspect. But why did he change his name and when? I drove to the Georgia motor vehicle office to see a copy of his driver's license. While I was there, I was standing next to a woman who was waiting to change her maiden name to her married name on her license. I said out loud to myself, "Damn. How in the world did he change his name?"

"He could have posted his name in the local newspaper to be contested." Said the woman.

I turned to her and said thank you. I left and went to the local newspaper location, and just like that, he had it in the paper for anyone to contest against him changing his name from Greg Smith to Andre Brown. I got him! But again why? I sat on the plane heading back to New York with two issues to deal with. The first was this was my only male cousin left in my family. What happens if I put him in prison? Would this destroy my family? My second issue was he was a detective who, from what I have learned, never did anything wrong on the job. I will be bringing down a detective the city and state really needed. Nonetheless, I was ready to inform my captain of my findings and ready to place Andre Brown under arrest. The next day I sat with my captain in his office.

"Cap. My suspect is Detective Andre Brown from the Hartford homicide squad."

"We are arresting a cop?"

"Yes. Here are my notes and paperwork."

He looked at them.

"This is a highly decorated detective with a clean record. Are we one hundred percent certain about this?"

"I am."

"Fine. Take your partner and make the arrest quietly and at his home."

I went to our desk and looked at Detective Whitehead.

"We're going to Connecticut to arrest the Ricardo Desire's murder suspect."

"Let's go."

Weeks after we arrested Detective Andre Brown, he remained in jail until his trial. I knew both cases were connected, so I started focusing on James's case. I saw my captain walking through the hallway, and I stopped him to provide an update.

"Good morning, captain. Since we're waiting for Detective Andre Brown's trial to start, I will be focusing on James Smith's cold case."

He looked at me with a "what the hell?" face.

"Jackson. I told you to sit on this Detective Andre Brown's case. Leave the Smith's cold case alone. It's a dead case. Shit!"

He walked away mumbling, and I couldn't believe he wanted me to stay on this case. I know it's important, but I could've been solving other cases. Months went by, and the trial started. Then came the day Daniel Scott testified. As I sat and listened to Daniel tell his story about Ricardo, I remembered this wasn't my main case I wanted to close. I was really tired of James's case hanging over my head. But that all changed seconds later when Daniel spoke about Double D, a.k.a. Diane Downs. I got up, left the courtroom, and called my partner.

"Meet me at the office. We're about to find Diane Downs."

"I already located her. Her last known address is in the Bronx. Come get me."

I met with him, and we drove up to the Bronx. We knocked on her door, and a young boy opened the door. He was around ten years old.

"Hello, handsome young man. Is your mommy or daddy home?"

"My mother went to heaven, and my daddy is on the couch."

Then we heard a strong male voice. "Who the hell is that, boy?"

"Sir, it's the police. My name is Detective Olena Jackson, and this is my partner Detective Donnie Whitehead. We like to ask you a few questions about—"

"I know what you are here for. About time y'all came. I've been waiting for y'all."

"Excuse me, sir?" Detective Whitehead said.

"Come on in and have a seat. Excuse the mess. My girl died five years ago. She killed herself because of her guilt. She left a suicide note and a letter for the cops if they ever came to see her. Let me get it for y'all."

He left and came back with the letter.

"You know, earlier this month a thin White woman came here and told me she was a private investigator. I thought she was a cop. She showed me her identification and asked if Diane was here. I told her the same thing I told you and gave her the suicide note to read. She took a picture of it and thanked me for helping her."

"Sir. We need to see that paper."

"I threw it away after she left. I couldn't take it anymore. I was going to wait another month before I opened this letter and then destroy it, but y'all came at the right time."

He passed me the letter, and I proceeded to read Double D's confession and involvement with James's murder. Diane was close friends with James growing up until high school. Unfortunately, James introduced Diane to his friend Percy, who treated her badly. After that, Diane wanted revenge on James. She got involved with a guy named Douglass who was looking for someone to do a hit on James. Diane met with Daniel Scott, Douglass, Justice, and a woman named L Boogie in Prospect

Park. They proceeded to plan the hit on James, and James was killed. Years later L Boogie and Diane encountered each other at L Boogie's aunt's funeral, and that was when Diane learned L Boogie's real name was Laura Parker, now known as Laura Brown. We got her!

I passed the letter to my partner, and after he read it, we thanked her boyfriend, kept the letter, and said our goodbyes. I waited for the next day and went to ADA Becks's office before court, but he wasn't there. I raced over to the courthouse, and before he could cross-examine Laura Brown, I gave him the letter, and I walked back and took a seat. Then the judge called for a recess.

"How did you get this?" ADA Becks asked.

"Detective Whitehead and I remembered Daniel Scott's testimony regarding Double D. We found her last address and talked with her boyfriend, who told us she killed herself five years ago. He welcomed us into his apartment and told us that he had a sealed envelope with her handwriting on it saying, *Only for the police to read!* This is the letter that was in it."

I handed ADA Becks the letter, then I and Detective Whitehead left, grabbed lunch, and waited in our car until it was time to return to the courtroom. The next day right after the verdict we knew we were robbed. I went straight home and thought about my dysfunctional family. The next morning ADA Becks called me.

"Good morning, Detective Jackson. We're going to arrest Laura Brown this morning for conspiracy to commit murder. Do you want to come?"

"As long as I'm not the one throwing on the cuffs, I will be there."

Within two hours, he picked me up, and we went to Connecticut. We had a local cop car with two officers meet us there. Again, I was back at my cousin's home for another arrest. One of the officers knocked on the door, and there was no answer. The other officer banged on the door.

"This is the police! Open up! We have an arrest warrant for Laura Brown."

A neighbor came out and walked over to me and ADA Becks.

"They are home. Their girls spent the night over here and are upstairs with my daughters. Laura and Andre wanted alone time last night."

Then we heard a broken glass sound, and one of the officers yelled, "Detective Jackson. ADA Becks. Come see this."

We swiftly walked around to the back of the house and through the back door. Laura was lying on the floor with her throat cut ear to ear. I fell back against one of the walls in the room.

Andre wasn't there, but he left a note stating,

I had to do it. She killed my brother!

About the Authors

Christina S. Sledge & Edward L. Sledge Jr.

Christina and Edward are the authors of *The Story of Christina and I* and *Ricardo's Collisions*. They have been happily married for more than twenty-one years. Born and raised in Brooklyn, NY, Christina received an undergraduate degree from Temple University and a graduate degree from The George Washington University. Edward is a disabled U.S. Army veteran. He received an undergraduate degree from Georgia Southern University and a graduate degree from Towson University. They started Sledge House Media in 2021.

For speaking engagements and to contact them:
   www.sledgehousemedia.com
   Instagram: @sledgehousemedia
   Twitter: Sledge House Media @house_sledge